To Ellie —

ALL I WANT FOR CHRISTMAS...IS MY SISTER'S BOYFRIEND

BROOKE BLAINE
ELLA FRANK

Dear Santa —
that one!

—♡— Brooke Blaine

COPYRIGHT

CHAPTER ONE

MILES

"AN 'I FLEXED and the Sleeves Fell Off' shirt for Rick...a Sriracha crate for your dad...a grilled cheese maker for Beth...and a wine glass that holds an entire bottle of wine for your mom." Holly Clark laughed as she shook her head, her dark brown curls swaying as she closed my shopping bag and set it on the chair beside her. "Please explain why anyone would need a grilled cheese maker. That's, like, the easiest thing in the world."

"You don't remember the time Beth set the kitchen on fire making cookies? I don't blame you for blocking it out. I'm still traumatized," I said, picking up my glass of hot buttered rum and taking a long, throat-warming sip. It was a holiday tradition, Christmas shopping with my best friend and devouring copious amounts of the delicious beverage and The Clove's famous gingerbread loaves—you know, *after* we'd spent almost all our money on gifts.

"Then hey, genius: maybe giving Beth something for the kitchen wasn't the smartest idea. I can't imagine she actually asked for something to help her burn the house down. Is this some kind of new McAllister family gag gift Christmas?"

I held up my hand in a Boy Scout's salute—it didn't matter that

I was never a Boy Scout, right? "I swear they all mentioned those things at some point this year. Although, I might've added some, uh...*interesting* additions."

"Oh no." Holly dug back into the bag, and when she pulled out one of the books, the horrified expression on her face made me almost spew my drink. "*What's Your Poo Telling You?* Oh my God. Miles, please tell me you aren't giving this to your parents."

"Bathroom reading material at its finest. My dad'll love it."

She shoved the book back into the bag. "That is so wrong."

"It's so right. Admit it: you want one."

"Not for Christmas!"

"More appropriate for a birthday gift opened in front of all your friends?"

Holly rolled her eyes and groaned. "You're hopeless. Tell you what, how about we don't exchange gifts this year."

"Too late. I already got you the perfect gift."

"Take it back, then."

"No way. Do you know how hard it was to track down a working banana phone?"

"A banana ph—" Holly snapped her mouth shut and lifted her hand to get the waiter's attention. "Could we get the check, please? My friend's lost his mind. I think it might be fatal."

Chuckling, I broke off a piece of the last gingerbread loaf and popped it in my mouth. She was complaining now, but she'd be grateful for an actual gift to unwrap, and come on, the banana phone was awesome.

"By the way, what did you get for the white elephant gift for Zack's party?" she asked.

"The... Aw, man. Nothing. I forgot."

Holly smiled triumphantly as she stole the last of the ginger-bread. "Guess that means I'm all done and you're a slacker. Pay up."

She got a special Miles death glare for about five seconds before I groaned and pulled my wallet out of my pocket. Also a tradition—a really stupid one, I was beginning to think—was that whoever finished their shopping last bought dinner. And here I thought I'd had this in the bag.

After I begrudgingly paid the waiter, we left and Holly linked her arm with mine.

"Since you're into the ridiculous this year, what about something like that?" She pointed to a novelty store with a huge leg lamp display straight out of *A Christmas Story.*

"Not bad, Clark," I said, veering us in that direction. "Not bad at all."

$\mathcal{T}$WENTY MINUTES LATER, we stood in the middle of the crowded store, other customers bumping past us every five seconds as I debated my options.

"What do you think?" I held up two boxes. "Shot glass roulette or a hard cider kit?"

Holly wrinkled her pert nose. "Neither?"

"Not helpful." I looked at my narrowed down choices and was about to bust out "eeny meeny miny mo" when Holly said, "The roulette's cheaper."

"Then roulette it is." I put back the hard cider kit and shot her a wink. "See? *That* was helpful."

"Speaking of helpful, remind me which wrapping paper you use so I don't pick your gift."

I grinned. "Deal."

Before I could move in the direction of the checkout, a hard shove from behind knocked me into the display, sending boxes of roulette kits flying and nearly knocking me off my feet. Whoever said the holidays brought out the best in people clearly hadn't been to the mall a week before Christmas.

When I righted myself with Holly's help, I turned around, fully prepared to let the inconsiderate jackass have it—

"Are you okay? I'm sorry, this place is a madhouse."

My whole body went still as I gazed up at the man with the smooth-as-whiskey voice. Taller than me by a good three inches, and with a head full of thick black hair someone would be lucky to run their fingers through, the...err...inconsiderate jackass just so happened to also be the most gorgeous man I'd ever seen in my life.

"Are you okay?" he asked again, but then he jerked forward slightly as a group of laughing teenaged girls, oblivious to anyone around them, moved past us. His arm went up in front of me, as if on instinct, to block me from getting bumped into...again.

Swoon. I'm officially swooning.

"I'm..." I blinked, hardly able to form a coherent sentence while his dark eyes were trained so intensely on mine. "I-it's fine. I'm fine."

One of his eyebrows arched, and then those gorgeous eyes of his swept over me, and as they did, I felt it every-freakin'-where. When he was done with his perusal, his gaze met mine again. "You are that."

I completely blanked then. Brain gone, breathing faint, voice nonexistent. He was beautiful.

"I don't know about you, but I think I might stick to online shopping next year," he said, a crooked smile turning up his lips, which, of course, my eyes zeroed in on and couldn't stop staring at.

Stop looking at his lips. Stop that. Stop iiit.

"Shot roulette, huh?" He nodded to the box in my hands, and heat flooded my face.

"Oh, it's not mine," I said, automatically tucking the package behind my back. "I mean, it's not for me. It's a gift. For someone else. Who's not me."

Obviously, I thought, wanting to bang my head against the wall. Geez, when had I turned into a bumbling mess?

He chuckled and ran a hand over the light dusting of scruff covering his jaw. I tried not to lick my lips at the movement, but I couldn't seem to be held entirely responsible for my actions at the moment. After all, he was dressed in business attire, a navy suit tailored to his tall, muscular frame, and heaven help me, that was my kryptonite.

"Well..." he trailed off.

"Well." Behind me, Holly poked my back furiously.

"I guess I'd better get back to shopping," he said. "Good luck with this crowd."

"Yeah, me too. I mean, you too." When I stumbled over my words, his smile only grew, and I wanted to whack myself over the head. Then he winked at me—unless that was some sort of eye twitch I was imagining—and walked away.

"Oh my God, oh my God, oh my God," Holly said, coming up beside me and squeezing my arm tight. "Miles, you have to go get his number. Did you see how he was checking you out? And he's so hot, like drop-dead, please-let-me-have-your-babies hot." When I didn't respond—because my tongue had lolled out like one of those Looney Tunes cartoons and I physically couldn't—she shook me. "Hello. Earth to Miles. He's getting away."

Swallowing, I looked down at the box in my hands. "I need to pay for this."

"*I'll* pay for this. You go."

"Go where?"

Holly stared at me like I'd gone completely brain-dead, which I supposed I had. "To talk to the hot guy. You barely said two words while he was trying to make conversation with you. You seriously need to work on your flirting skills."

"Why? He was just being nice."

"Nice? He eyed you like a delicious cut of steak."

"That's ridiculous. He was just checking that I didn't break any bones so I wouldn't sue him." I headed toward the register and got in line as Holly huffed behind me.

"Miles, have you looked in the mirror lately?"

"What?"

"Look, I'm not just saying that because I'm your best friend. If anything, I'd call you out for looking a hot mess. But...you've gotten pretty damn handsome lately."

I rolled my eyes. "Oh, please—"

"You've got this whole cute nerd thing going on with the

5

button-ups and corduroy pants. And this hair?" She reached up and mussed my brown waves. "Like, I can do this and it makes it look even better. I don't know how that's possible."

"It's called 'need a haircut.'"

"No, it's called 'get your butt out there and show that gorgeous specimen how hot you are.'"

"But—"

"No buts, McAllister."

I sighed and lifted up on my toes, doing a quick scan of the walkways outside the store, and felt a mixture of remorse and relief when I didn't see him. "He's already gone."

"Then go track him down."

"I'm not going to track him down."

"Yeah, because you're a chicken." She crossed her arms. "I can't believe you let him get away. He could've been the one."

"Sure he was."

After paying and adding another bag to my pile, we ventured out into the mall, which, even at the late hour, was still crammed full of people. A week until Christmas and all the last-minute shoppers were frantically pushing past each other to grab everything on their lists.

Lucky for me, I was finally done, which deserved a pat on the back...or maybe another one of those hot buttered rum drinks.

"So did we get everythi—" I started, but Holly gasped.

"Oh my God, look!" She grabbed my hand and dragged me over to the railing overlooking the first floor, her attention caught on something below. "Santa's still here and the line isn't insane."

"So?"

"So let's do it. We have to." She tugged on my hand, pulling me toward the escalator, but I stopped in my tracks.

"Whoa, whoa, whoa. You're not suggesting we go sit on Santa's freakin' lap, are you? Because I'm gonna have to pass."

Holly turned around, and when she saw I wasn't budging, her bottom lip popped out. "Miiiles, please? When was the last time you took a picture with Santa?"

"Uh, when I was eight and still believed he'd bring me a Tonka truck set for Christmas."

"And you got it, remember? You made me race you for three months straight."

"So?"

"Sooo, you should ask him for something you really want." She gave me a mischievous smile and nudged my side with her elbow. "You know. Like a boyfriend. The seriously hot one that you flubbed things up with a few minutes ago. He just might give it to you."

"Santa might give me a boyfriend? Wrapped up in a bow under the tree and everything?" I gasped and put my hand over my heart.

"Don't make fun."

"Aren't we a little old to still believe in Santa?"

"Twenty-five isn't old. Besides, we're still kids at heart."

"Ugh. That might be the cheesiest thing I've ever heard you say."

"Oh, come on, Miles, it's Christmas. Like the one time of year we're allowed to be super cheesy and watch all the awesome holiday Passionflix movies we want and listen to 'I Want a Hippopotamus for Christmas' nonstop without anyone judging us."

"But—"

"But nothing. You're doing this with me, Miles Graham McAllister, so you might as well embrace it."

I let out a low whistle as I threw an arm over her shoulders. "Using my full name to get what you want now, huh?"

"Hey, I'm not above bribery either if that's what it takes."

I didn't doubt that for a second, just like I knew there was no way I was getting out of this without making a run for it.

"Okay, fine," I said. "But I wouldn't do this for anyone else—"

Holly shrieked and wrapped her arms tight around my waist. "Yaaaay. This is why I keep you around."

"That and I pay half the rent," I teased.

Her chocolate-brown eyes sparkled at me. "That too."

7

Holly walked us over to the escalator, and as we rode it down to the first floor, I eyed the scene before us. The elaborate setup that served as Santa's workshop had ten-foot flocked Christmas trees, overflowing with ornaments, standing tall on either side of the huge red and gold throne Santa sat on. His elves were busy tending to the customers and attempting to make the children in line and in his lap smile.

Man, I would not want that job.

Santa's hearty laugh brought my attention back to the man sitting in the middle of the action, and I had to admit the mall had done a good job picking out the guy. Rosy cheeks, glasses perched low on his nose, and a round belly filling out his red-and-white jacket and trousers. A toddler sat in his lap now, with a small hand wrapped around his long white beard, and when the little girl tugged, the white curls, surprisingly, didn't fall down his face. Huh. Maybe he prepped all year for this by growing it out.

As we joined the short line, one of the elves made their way over to us, looking entirely too perky for what had to be an exhausting day of dealing with people. Or maybe that was my exhaustion talking. Shopping was hard work, and my bed was calling.

"Both of you together?" the elf asked, not seeming surprised in the least to see two twenty-somethings in line to see Santa—which made me feel slightly less absurd.

"Yes, please," Holly said, practically bouncing on her toes. We chose the package we wanted and each handed over a ten-dollar bill. "This is so much fun. What should I ask for?"

We looked at each other at the same time and said together: "A new job."

Laughing as we moved up the line, I nodded. "Definitely a new job. And a sexy boss."

"I don't need a sexy boss to distract me."

"I didn't mean for him to distract *you*."

"Ooooh," she said, catching my drift. "Okay, so a job for me and a sexy boss as eye candy for you. Got it."

"Actually...the likelihood of Santa delivering a person on Christmas is pretty low. I think I'll ask for a new car instead."

"From Tonka trucks to new cars. We don't ask for much, do we?"

"Hey, you started this."

The line moved quickly, and before I knew it, we were next. One of the elves smiled at us and led us down the candy-cane-lined walkway toward Santa's chair. Although, as we approached, I realized it wasn't a chair at all, but an oversized throne that made anyone sitting in it look smaller than he really was. In reality, Santa was a tall, sturdy man, which was a good thing, since he'd have to hold the weight of both of us.

His blue eyes twinkled as he watched us climb the stairs, and a loud, jolly *ho ho ho* boomed out of him, causing Holly to startle beside me.

"Miles McAllister and Holly Clark," Santa said, spreading his hands wide. "Come up here and tell Santa what he can do for you."

Holly's eyes went wide as she gaped at him. "How'd you know our names?"

Because his elves told him, I was about to say, but Santa beat me to it.

"Santa knows all," he said, winking, and then he patted his thighs. "Sit, sit."

Holly was quick to obey, perching on his left leg, while I carefully took a seat on his right.

"I hope we don't break your lap," I joked, making sure not to put my full weight on him. Big guy or not, he probably had to ice his thighs every night.

"Don't worry. No need to be shy," Santa said, patting me on the back like he knew what I was thinking. "Have you both been good boys and girls this year?"

"Oh. Uh..." Holly looked at me with apprehension in her eyes, like she hadn't been expecting that question and didn't want to be quite that honest with Santa, and I chuckled.

"Define good," I said.

Another *ho ho ho* rumbled out of Santa. "Ah, I remember how it is at your age. Not to worry. Neither of you are on my naughty list."

"Really?" Holly said, surprised, and then she shook it away and sat up taller. "I mean, of course we're not."

I smirked as one of the elves waved to get our attention for the photo. Knowing if I ruined the picture, Holly would probably disown me, I straightened and smiled brightly, but let it drop as soon as we got a thumbs-up. Man, if my brother ever got hold of the evidence, he'd never let me live this down.

"Holly," Santa boomed, "what is it you'd like this Christmas?"

It was like a sudden bout of shyness overcame my best friend as she peeked up at Santa from under her lashes. "Well, if it's not too much to ask, I'd really, really love a new job. Something in fashion, preferably, but really anything that doesn't include getting coffee for my horrible bosses ten times a day."

Santa chuckled. "Ah yes. Your bosses are on my naughty list, so I think I might be able to put in a good word for you elsewhere, Holly."

"Really?" She beamed. "Thank you, Santa. Oh, and if the new job can pay a little better too, that'd be amazing."

He let out another belly laugh. "Is that all?" When she nodded, Santa turned his attention to me. "And for you, Miles? What can Santa bring you?"

With the sincere, open expression on his face, you'd almost believe he could give you whatever your heart desired. But I wasn't a kid anymore, and I didn't believe in silly things like Santa and a bunch of magical elves and reindeer, no matter how cool I'd thought they were growing up.

"I, uh, don't really need anything," I said.

"No? Maybe there's something you want, then? Anything at all."

I'd opened my mouth to speak when my eyes caught on a tall, dark-haired man moving through the crowd. My heart skipped a beat—hell, several beats—as the gorgeous guy from my store run-in stopped outside a candle shop maybe twenty feet away.

Oh no. If he saw me sitting on Santa's lap, that would be it for me. I'd die right then and there from embarrassment.

"Miles," Holly said, and then flicked my knee to get my attention, but I was too focused on my new crush, if only to make sure he didn't look my way. *Please don't look this way.*

I vaguely heard Holly apologize before saying, "Miles would like a boyfriend."

"Holls!" I jerked my head in her direction, and she gave an innocent shrug.

"Mmm, is that true, Miles?" Santa asked. "Would you like someone special to spend your Christmases with?"

"I mean...doesn't everyone?" I glanced back over to the candle shop, but, just my luck, he was no longer standing there. Great. I'd lost him. Again.

"Or maybe there's someone in particular you've got your eye on?" Santa's gaze followed mine, and when I turned my head toward him, Santa gave me a knowing smile.

"Well, we'll just see what I can do for you, shall we?" he said, that twinkle in his eye making my stomach flip with nervous anticipation. Which was crazy, because it wasn't like either of our wishes would be coming true. He was a mall Santa, not the real thing. Basically the equivalent of a pop-up shop psychic hired to entertain. A fake.

"Yeah, sure. You do that," I said, getting to my feet. I was ready to get out of there. Especially before gorgeous guy came back and I was busted asking Santa for Christmas wishes.

"One more thing, Miles." Santa motioned for me to come closer, and when I reluctantly leaned in, he said, "You might want to rethink your sister's gift. Or just...keep an eye on her."

My eyes widened, and I jolted back so fast that I nearly lost my footing on the stairs, but Holly was right there steadying me, her jaw on the ground, matching mine.

"Holy crap," she whispered.

How would this Santa guy know about my sister's gift? Maybe he had elves spying on people around the mall, eavesdropping on conversations. Yeah. That had to be it. What a scam.

"Now off you go," scam Santa said, giving us a cheerful wave. "Have a merry Christmas, Holly and Miles."

"Right." Holly recovered first and returned his wave. "Merry Christmas, Santa."

I narrowed my eyes on the old man, trying to figure out his game, but Holly's hold on my arm was firm and insistent. She dragged us down the path to where one of the elves held out our picture packet, and when we were out of earshot, she said, "Oh my *God*. Can you believe that?

I scoffed. "I know. What a bunch of crap."

"Wait, what? Crap?"

"Don't tell me you actually fell for all that."

"He knew about your sister!"

"Please. It was a lucky guess."

"No way. He was for real."

Sighing, I placed my hands on her shoulders. "Holls, I know you were named after Christmas and this is, like, your thing, but don't get your hopes up, okay? I mean, I hope you get a new job, but it'll be because you kick ass and not because some guy in a suit made it happen."

Holly pushed a brown curl away from her face and lifted her chin. "We'll see about that. Now come on, Grinch. Let's get home and start wrapping. But we're watching *The Trouble with Mistletoe*, and I don't want to hear a word about it."

"No complaints from me. The guy's hot." I grinned and took her bags, adding them to mine. A feeling of being watched prickled the back of my neck, and I looked over my shoulder to find Santa laughing, twin girls propped up on his lap. He inclined his head toward me and winked before turning his attention back to the little girls.

I frowned and turned away, and Holly and I trekked across the mall to where I'd parked earlier. The night had veered off into weird territory, but it was nothing late-night cocktails and eye candy wouldn't fix.

And speaking of eye candy... If "Santa" wanted to send the guy I'd run into earlier my way, who was I to complain?

Tell you what, "Santa." You put that guy under my Christmas tree this year, and I'll happily eat my words, I thought with a snort.

Yeah. Never. Gonna. Happen.

CHAPTER TWO

MILES

*T*HE NEXT NIGHT, Holly and I ventured off to Zack's annual holiday party. A heavy dusting of snow had swept over the city in the time since I'd gotten off work—my final nine-to-fiver before leaving for my parents' house tomorrow—but luck-ily, the party was only a short walk from our apartment. My fingers were crossed that the skies would clear by morning so I wouldn't have to drive in the mess.

Shivering and teeth chattering, we arrived at our destination, a twenty-story building on the busy corner of downtown Greene Street. Zack's father owned the independent hotel, so every year the party took place on the top floor, in the space usually reserved for meetings and conferences. And because Zack was a bigger fan of the holidays than Holly—or maybe it was just that he was a bigger partier—the room was always transformed into something straight out of a storybook. One year it was a winter wonderland, complete with snow blowers; another year there were life-size reindeer.

As we stepped on to the elevator, I nodded toward the bag Holly held. "So what did you end up going with for the white elephant exchange?"

"A bottle of Tequila Rose. I think our gifts are getting worse every year."

"Like our outfits," I said, looking down at the Grinch onesie I wore. We'd been told to dress up in 'Whoville-style pajamas,' whatever that meant, so Holly had grabbed an outfit for me while shopping for her own. So while I looked ridiculous in a fuzzy, bright green ensemble, she wore a short blond wig with a long pink Snuggie-looking dress...thing. Honestly, I had no idea what she was until I heard her tell a passerby she was "Cindy Lou Who." Right. I knew that.

When the elevator door opened, a Seussian snow-covered archway with "Welcome to Whoville" greeted us, and just beyond that, well...talk about overstimulation. Everywhere you looked there was tinsel and garland vying to see which one could decorate the most space, as well as oversized ball ornaments gleaming from the ceiling, lit by hundreds of twinkling multicolored lights. Whimsically decorated trees and cutouts of Whoville homes lined the perimeter of the room, and one of the trees even had a Grinch climbing inside. And in the center of the room, a massive tree stretched up to the ceiling, serving as the focal point.

"Wow," Holly said from beside me. "How did he even get that in here?"

"Welcome, welcome, Whoville-ians," Zack said, jumping out in front of us in a ta-da motion. *Good grief.* His hair had been sprayed grey and spread like the Red Sea to each side of his head, curling up in a loop, and he'd obviously used a professional for the facial prosthetics that gave him rounder cheeks and an upturned nose. "Mayor Augustus Mayhoo at your service. Pleased you could make it, Cindy Lou Who and, uh...I suppose you're allowed in, Grinch." He smirked and pulled me in for a hug before doing the same to Holly.

"This is unreal. I don't know how you manage to top yourself every year, but you do," Holly said.

"It's because I'm amazing. No need for modesty. Now, five-second tour: gifts can go under the tree, games are to the left, and refreshments are over by the Whoville Bakery. I recommend the Naughty Nutcracker. Has a bit of a kick." Zack turned to Holly. "Mind if I steal you away for a few? There's someone I want you to meet."

Holly raised her eyebrows my way and handed me her gift bag, and as Zack led her away, my lips quirked. My best friend never lacked for admirers, but it'd been a while since anyone worthy had managed to get her attention. It didn't help that they had to filter through me first. I wasn't about to let just anyone into our little circle.

There were already a ton of presents underneath the massive tree, and I had to walk around to the other side to find an open spot. I knelt down and sandwiched Holly's gift in so it sat upright, and as I placed my box in front of it, I heard a male say behind me, "I have a feeling I know what that is."

My hand froze at the familiar sound, though it wasn't because I knew the person well. It was because I'd been playing the short conversation from our run-in in my head over and over again since last night.

But no...it couldn't be him. There's no way he'd be here, at a random party downtown, the same one I was. Or could he?

I rose to my feet and turned around, and sure enough, there he was. Same gorgeous, thick black hair swept back off his face, same crooked smile turning up his full lips. The only difference tonight was that he'd traded in his suit for a pair of long-sleeved pajamas covered in candy canes and slippers. Somehow, he made even that look hot.

"H-hi," I managed.

"Hi." His smile grew. "Don't worry, I'll be careful not to knock you over this time."

Hey, I wouldn't be opposed to you knocking me into my headboard. No —shut up, Miles. Think of something else, like cookies or presents. Instead, I took one look at his outfit and blurted, "Your balls are impressive."

He let out a low chuckle. "Sorry?"

I pointed to the long flashing necklace he wore that was made out of Christmas ornamental balls and matched his pajamas. "Your, uh, necklace."

He glanced down, and as if he didn't know it was there, he said, "Oh. Right. Well, it's always important to make sure your balls are properly hung."

I chuckled. I had *not* been expecting that.

"I'm Aiden," he said, holding his hand out.

"Miles." I gave him what I hoped was a firm shake and not one that showed I was in any way flustered by touching him. His grip was strong and lingered as he smiled at me, and I liked the way it felt.

"It's nice to meet you, Miles."

I'd opened my mouth to respond when a blast came from beside us, startling us both and causing Aiden to drop my hand. The man on the unicycle continued to blow on his horn as he sped away through the crowd, and when I noticed Aiden's wide eyes, I laughed.

"First Zack party?" I said.

"It is."

"You should've been here when he reenacted Santa falling off the roof. I think everyone had a heart attack, but luckily, he'd landed on a mattress covered with snow."

"Terribly sorry I missed that," Aiden said, laughing. Then he cocked his head to the side, and the way he studied me sent a shiver to my core. "I was going to get something to drink if you'd like to join me?"

"Yeah, sure," I said, trying for nonchalant. Was Holly seeing this? I needed proof it was actually happening and not some figment of my imagination. "I heard the Naughty Nutcracker is not to be missed."

Aiden eyed me for a second, but then his lips quirked up at the sides. "If I didn't know any better, I'd think you were a little preoccupied with my balls, Miles."

"Well, they are nice balls."

Aiden chuckled and leaned closer to me, and Lord, the man smelled phenomenal—like snow, pine, and something delicious that I couldn't quite put my finger on. All I knew was I wanted to lick his neck.

"I'm glad you think so," Aiden said.

Really, could the man be any more perfect? Good-looking and a massive flirt to boot?

"So, what exactly is in a Naughty Nutcracker?"

I had no idea, really. But every time the guy said the word "nut," my mind went somewhere completely different than the drink.

"Miles?" Aiden said, and I mentally slapped myself back into the present.

Get yourself together, man, or he's going to think the Grinch stole your brain and not Christmas. "Sorry, I, um, didn't ask. But if Zack's recommending it, I'd caution moderation. That guy has no limitations when it comes to alcohol."

"Oh? Know this from experience, do you?"

"Let's just say I'll never take another Scroogedriver from him again. And if he offers you one, just say no. You'll thank me for it later."

"Good to know," Aiden said. "But now I'm curious what happened to make you issue a PSA against it."

"My lips are sealed," I said, finding it surprisingly easy to talk to him.

Aiden's eyes dropped to my mouth. "That sure would be a shame."

I cleared my throat, knowing if I didn't give myself something to do, and quickly, I just might end up dragging this dreamboat away and doing *him* instead.

"So um...about that drink," I said, and gestured over my shoulder. "We should go track it down."

"I'd love to."

This guy really was everything I had ever wished for, and I was starting to think I needed to go find Holly and thank her for making me sit my ass on Santa's lap this year. "Okay then, follow me. Zack said it's over by the bakery."

As I walked off through the crowd, I wasn't sure if I was imagining it, but I swore I could feel Aiden's eyes on my ass. Suddenly I wished I'd made him go ahead, because I had no doubt he was just as fine going as he was coming. *I'd have to be sure to check that out later...*

We made our way through the crowd to the back, where a long bar was being tended to by a handful of Whoville-ians. As Aiden and I sidled up to an open spot, I picked up the specialty cocktail list.

"A Three Wise Men shot? Oh God. I did one of those on my twenty-first birthday, and never again." I groaned. "It was three shot glasses, and one had whiskey, one had bourbon, and the other had scotch, and I had to do them, bam, bam, bam, no chaser. Worst hangover ever."

"Ouch. I think I'll pass on that one."

"Uh, yeah. Unless you want to forget tonight ever happened."

"I definitely don't want to forget tonight."

I swallowed hard at the way he looked at me and dropped my gaze back down to the list in my hand. How anyone could stay upright under that potent stare was beyond me. "Um... It looks like a Naughty Nutcracker is Kahlua, Grand Marnier, Baileys Irish Cream, and amaretto over ice. I hope you have a sweet tooth."

"I'm suddenly developing one." Aiden caught the attention of one of the bartenders. "Two Naughty Nutcrackers, please."

"Excellent choice," she said, and went off to make our drinks.

"So, are you from around here?" I asked. "I've never seen you before and now I've run into you twice."

"Maybe that's fate."

"Maybe that's not an answer."

Aiden let out a low laugh. "I moved here a few months ago from Baltimore."

"For work?"

"Not completely. I thought a fresh start would be nice. What about you?"

"I grew up a few hours from here, but I went to college at Stoneyside and decided to stay after I graduated."

"And how recently was that?"

It was obvious to me that Aiden was a bit older than I was... late twenties, maybe? Thirty? I'd always been told I looked young for my age—I blamed that on not being able to bulk up much, no matter how much protein powder I consumed—and the last thing I wanted was for him to think I was some fresh-out-of-college guy with no experience.

"About three and a half years ago," I said.

"Which makes you, what, twenty-five or so?"

"Yep. How old are you?"

Aiden rubbed his finger along his lower lip. "How old do you think I am? Be kind."

"And if I'm not?"

My teasing made Aiden's grin grow, as the bartender set a couple of old-fashioned glasses in front of us.

"Two Naughty Nutcrackers for two naughty Whoville-ians," she said, before moving on to the next customer.

Aiden handed me a glass and picked one up for himself. "Tell you what. If you guess correctly, I'll do one of those horrible Three Wise Men shots."

"And if I'm wrong?"

"Then you're gonna help me find the mistletoe."

There was no way I was going to say no to that. If anyone was going to benefit from that piece of kiss-inspiring vegetation, it was going to be me. "Just help you find it?"

Aiden raised his glass, took a sip, and then said, "Guess, and you'll find out."

God, he was sexy, and I was well, more...cute? I'd always been the *aww, isn't he adorable* guy, and people like Aiden didn't usually mix with people like me—until, apparently, now. If this really was Santa's doing, he had hit this one out of the park, and I was not about to blow it. *Well, er, at least not right this second.*

"Um, okay, let's see," I said, and then let my eyes travel down his ornament pajamas—because, let's be real, I wasn't stupid. I then raised my eyes to his smirking lips and guessed, "Twenty-eight?"

"You know, I actually think you gave that a fair shot..."

"Of course I did. I want to see you swallow back those three men."

Aiden let out a loud, boisterous laugh and took a step closer to me. "You seem to have a one-track mind tonight, Miles. That's why I'm shocked you actually took a fair go at this."

"I don't know what's wrong with my mouth tonight." Knowing full well that *he* was exactly what was wrong with it. One look at him and all I'd wanted was to drag him off somewhere dark and private.

"Absolutely nothing wrong from what I can see," he said.

Jesus, he was too much—and I loved it.

"Although, I'm about to find out for sure when I get you under the mistletoe. Aren't I?"

"I guessed wrong?" *Oh darn, what a terrible tragedy, having to find a mistletoe with this man.*

"Mhmm." Aiden took another swallow of his drink, and I followed suit, my mouth suddenly dry. "Twenty-nine."

I'd been close, but thankfully not close enough. While it would've been entertaining to watch him shudder through the Three Wise Men shot, it would be much more entertaining to help him find the mistletoe.

When Aiden finished off his drink, I realized I'd been nursing mine and quickly downed a mouthful. It was pretty good, actually, deceivingly sweet knowing how strong it really was. When I was done, I set my empty glass on the bar beside Aiden's, and then he surprised the hell out of me by grabbing my hand.

"You ready?" he asked.

Uh, yeah, I am. He was lucky I wasn't climbing on his back.

I nodded and gave his hand a squeeze, and he responded by lacing our fingers and squeezing mine back. Something so simple, but it made my pulse race. It was crazy, since what did I even know about this guy other than the handful of things I'd learned tonight, but as impulsive as it was, it all felt...magical. Like one of those Christmas movies Holly and I watched during the holidays, the ones that gave you all the feels and also made you a little bit hot under the collar. That was exactly how I felt holding Aiden's hand as I walked alongside him, and in that moment, I was convinced I would go anywhere with him.

I pointed up at a greenery bunch hanging over one of the Whoville doorways. "Is that mistletoe?"

Aiden squinted at it. "Nope."

We walked some more, and I tugged him back when I saw another bunch strung up over the dancefloor, but this one had red berries on it. "What about that?"

"I think that's just holly."

"You have a lot of experience with this, huh?"

Aiden glanced over his shoulder. "I've watched my fair share of Christmas movies. I know how this works."

Before I could reply, he was off again, weaving us through the crowds of people drinking and laughing, and I had to admit that I was feeling slightly lightheaded from how eager Aiden seemed to track down this spot and get me under it—that or it was the Naughty Nutcracker kicking in. Either way, I could feel my heart thumping in time with the synthesizers of "Wonderful Christmas-time" as we entered the next room, where the only lights on were those wrapped around the two trees by a set of doors leading to a balcony.

"Maybe we should look for the people kissing," I joked, as Aiden headed toward the doors, and as we got closer, I noticed that was exactly what he'd just spotted.

Out on the balcony terrace, there were colorful twinkle lights strung up, illuminating the area that had been decked out in a winter wonderland with the falling snow, and as we stepped out onto it, the couple who had been wrapped around one another passed us by. The girl was rosy-cheeked and grinning as her man led her back inside, and it was easy to see the ambiance and magic of the night had swept them up in its embrace—much like it had me.

She giggled as they passed by, and as she looked up at me, I felt a sense of kinship with her. Like we were sharing a secret moment. One where we knew exactly what the other had just done and was about to do, and I had a feeling I'd be grinning as widely as her within the next few minutes or so. Fingers crossed.

As Aiden and I stepped out onto the balcony, it was as though we stepped into another world. The doors blocked the chatter and music from inside, and it was just me and Aiden.

"I believe we've found it," Aiden said as he drew me to a stop in the center of the balcony where the lights met, then he looked up and pointed. "I told you I know how this works."

I didn't know if it was the alcohol thrumming through my veins, or if it was pent-up desire, but I found myself stepping closer to Aiden. With our hands still linked, we stood toe to toe, so close I could taste the puffs of air he exhaled. I wanted more of that sweetness, but I wanted his next breath to be joined with mine.

"Then why don't you show me?" I said.

That must've been what he wanted to hear, because Aiden's fingers tightened around mine, bringing me in closer. He held our joined hands at his waist as his other came up to cup my jaw, and then his thumb brushed against my lower lip.

Just that touch and I felt it everywhere. It was like we were in our own little snow globe with the way the snowflakes fell softly around us and clung to his dark lashes. He was simply gorgeous, and as he lowered his head, I moved up onto my toes, wanting nothing more than to get closer to the mouth I'd been looking at for the last half hour.

"Fate..." Aiden whispered against my lips, and a shiver raced up my spine. "That's what running into you tonight is. Fate."

My lips parted, and as I was about to respond, he gently grazed his over mine, and I trembled. What was going on here? I'd

23

thought this was going to be a quick, fiery kiss we'd joke about and possibly repeat several times if I was lucky. But this was so much more. My knees felt weak, and as the warmth of his lips pressed a little firmer against mine, I reached up and grabbed at his arm to keep myself steady.

The air outside was crisp and cool, but right then I could've been standing in front of a blazing fire with the flames now licking through my veins, and when the tip of his tongue traced my lower lip, begging for entrance, a moan escaped my throat before I could stop it.

A deep-throated rumble left Aiden, and before I could even try to get my brain to catch up, his tongue entered my mouth and erased every other kiss I'd ever had from my mind.

My fingers dug into his arm, as he trailed his down my throat and around to the back of my neck, and when he threaded them through my hair and angled his head to get a deeper taste, I just about melted into a puddle at his feet.

This kiss was way beyond anything I'd expected when he suggested we find the mistletoe, and when he smiled against my lips, and then nipped my lower one, I found myself close to begging him not to stop.

"I have definitely developed a sweet tooth tonight, Miles. And it's a craving I don't think will be satisfied with just one kiss. Can I see you again?"

"Yes—" I started, as the doors busted open and a mass of party-goers flooded onto the balcony, breaking us apart and invading our private moment. Without the warmth of his body pressed against mine, I quivered in the cold, missing his touch already.

"Aiden, my man," Zack shouted as he wrapped an arm around Aiden's shoulders. "I've been looking for you. We need shots. Drinks and shots. Shots and drinks."

Aiden caught my eyes. "Actually, I—"

"Hey, Miles, you come too," Zack said, waving me over, and then, with his arm still around Aiden, he started back inside, the crowd parting for them easily. Aiden glanced over his shoulder, and

I nodded, heading in their direction, though no one was moving aside for me.

I'd just made it off the balcony when I felt a tug on my arm and turned around to find Holly, her eyes wide, and her dark skin pale —and not from the cold.

"What's wrong?" I asked, pulling her to the side out of the way off the people heading outside.

"We have to leave," she said, panic in her voice.

"Leave? But we just got here, and you're not gonna believe this, but I've been hanging out with the guy from—"

"Miles, Scott's here."

Oh shit. Of anything she could've said, that was the last thing I wanted to hear, and all because I knew what it meant. Remember when I said Holly didn't lack for admirers? Let's just say there'd been a rotten one in the bunch, one she'd almost had to file a restraining order against, and though he'd long since left town, there was no way she needed to be anywhere near that guy.

But...

I stood on my tiptoes, looking in the direction of the bar for Aiden. I didn't want to leave, not after the best kiss of my life, but I wouldn't leave my friend in a bad situation either, and Holly was my family. She'd never think twice if the roles were reversed.

Aiden and Zack weren't at the bar, and as I searched the room, I couldn't find them anywhere.

"Miles, please, I don't want him to see me," Holly said, angling herself behind me, with her back to the wall.

"We're going," I said, giving the room one last look and feeling the disappointment settle in the pit of my stomach when I still didn't see Aiden.

Okay... I couldn't tell him goodbye, but I *could* get his number from Zack. I mean, he'd asked to see me again, so surely this wasn't a one-night deal.

As I kept a lookout for Scott, I steered Holly toward the elevator we'd come up on and told myself I would see Aiden again.

Because like he'd said: this had been fate...right?

CHAPTER THREE

MILES

*N*O SUCH LUCK with the weather the next day. It snowed the entire drive back to Wiltshire, which took six hours instead of the usual four. Luckily, I was carpooling with Holly, since her family lived a couple of doors down from mine.

"Can I just say again that I'm so, so sorry I made you leave last night. If I'd known you saw dreamy mall guy again—"

"Aiden," I interjected.

"Right, Aiden. If I'd known he was there, I would've just walked myself home."

"Downtown? In the middle of the night? By yourself?"

"Okay, so maybe I would've just hidden in the bathroom all night."

I gave her the side-eye and flipped on my blinker to exit the freeway. Only a few more miles and we'd be home. I was ready to stretch my legs and steal a few cookies I knew would be waiting for me on Mom's kitchen counter.

"It's fine, Holls. Zack knows him, so I'm sure I'll see him again." *Especially after that kiss.* I barely slept last night, reliving it over and over.

"I bet he tracks you down and calls *you*."

"Yeah, okay," I said, but inside I thrilled at the possibility. I could still feel the way my insides had completely flipped over on themselves when he looked at me, not to mention the way I'd melted when his lips had pressed against mine.

"Stop doing that," Holly said, and shoved me in the arm.

"What?"

"Doubting yourself. I can hear it in your voice. Did I or did I not tell you that you were looking cuter and cuter these days, Miles? I'm telling you, he *will* call."

I sure hoped so. But as much as I wanted to leave it up to Aiden's precious fate, I knew the second the holidays were over I'd be on the phone with Zack tracking down that man's number.

"Okay, enough about that," I said. "You know I have to mentally prepare myself for holidays with the family, so stop distracting me and help me focus."

Holly grinned, her beautiful, bright smile lighting her entire face as she no doubt recalled some of the past mayhem that had taken place at the McAllister household. "Especially with Rick back home this year."

Rick had been deployed overseas last year and things just hadn't felt the same without him. But having him back with us this year would certainly bring back the chaos we were all used to when he was around.

"God help us. But at least my parents will likely focus on him instead of harassing Beth about freezing her eggs."

"That's too much pressure. If I were Beth, I'd tell them to mind their own business."

I snorted. "Sure you would."

"Okay, well I'd definitely be thinking it."

The familiar sign for the Twelve Oaks neighborhood came into view, and as I turned onto the street we'd grown up on, the rush of nostalgia hit, as it always did when I came back for a visit. Not much had changed since my last trip home, although it would be hard to tell if it had due to the blanket of fresh snow covering everything in sight. Tonight, most of the houses here would be lit up with twinkling lights, my family's included.

I turned into the Clarks' driveway and popped the trunk before getting out to help unload Holly's bag. She came around the car at the same time as me, and together we heaved her thousand-pound suitcase out of the trunk. Honest to God, it was like she packed bricks instead of clothes.

"Thanks for driving," she said, giving me a hug. "I'll come by later. Tell your parents I said hi and to lay off Beth."

"Hah, yeah, right. Let your mom know I'll be by to steal some rocky road."

"Will do."

She waved as I got back in the car and drove down to my parents' driveway a couple of doors down. Looked like I was the last to arrive, as Rick's truck, and Beth's apparently new car took up the spots behind Mom and Dad's, leaving mine to squeak in almost onto the street.

I'd barely gotten my small rolling suitcase out when the front door opened and I heard my mom squeal.

"Hey, baby boy," she called out, waving her arms. "Do you need some help?"

"Nah, I got it. Stay inside." It was cold out, and the wind was beginning to pick up. I wrapped my scarf around my neck and tucked my head into it as I strode up the sidewalk.

"You made it," Mom said, pulling me in for an embrace before I'd even gotten my bag onto the porch. I steadied it beside me and wrapped my arms around her waist, breathing in the scent of sugar that always reminded me of her and served as proof there would indeed be her famous chocolate minty melt cookies waiting inside. "How was the drive?"

"Not too bad. I drove slow, promise."

"That's my boy," she said, stepping back so she could get a good look at me. "Oh dear. You're looking too thin. Get inside. I made a plate of minty melts just for you."

"You love me. You really love me," I said, grinning and rolling my suitcase inside.

It never ceased to amaze me how all-out my parents went for the holidays. Fresh garland wound its way around the banister leading upstairs and also flowed down from the fireplace mantel and basically everywhere it possibly could. Mom's massive collection of nutcrackers were featured around the living room in special niches she'd made just for them as though they lived there year-round, and off in the back corner of the space stood the eight-foot spruce Christmas tree.

"The place looks wonderful, Mom," I said as I let go of my bag and unwound my scarf. She turned to look at the living room where the five stockings we had made years ago when we were children were hanging neatly in a row off the fireplace.

"It does, doesn't it? It's only missing one thing, but we're working on that now."

I frowned as she took my hand, leading me inside toward the tree. "I don't know. It looks perfect to me." Really, the place could be in a magazine, it was so festive.

"No, no," she said as she patted my hand. "The lights on the tree went out just a few minutes ago, and you can't have a Christmas tree without lights. But lucky for us, Beth's boyfriend is checking it out."

I stopped in my tracks to look down at my mom, and raised an eyebrow. "Beth's boyfriend? I didn't even know she *had* a boyfriend."

Mom beamed at me and nodded. "Neither did I. That girl, she's so tight-lipped about these things."

"Maybe she just wanted to surprise you."

"Well, it's a lovely surprise. He's just a dream. Why don't you come in here and I'll introduce you?"

As we walked into the living room, I spotted my brother sitting on the couch, his phone in hand, texting away to someone, and as we came up behind him, he quickly shoved it down beside his leg.

"'Bout time you finally got here, brother," Rick said as he got to his feet. An inch or so shorter than me, Rick was built like a bull—muscles upon muscles. His hair was still shaved close to his head, true military style, and when Mom let me go so I could hug him, I didn't even care that it felt like he was gonna crush every bone in my body. It was just so good to see him.

"Yeah, it took a little longer thanks to this awesome weather. Really, it couldn't have waited one more day."

"No shit. I have a feeling we'll be getting a few good workouts over the next few days shoveling the walkway for Mom."

Ugh. That was so not a chore I enjoyed. It was right behind chopping firewood.

"I promise to make it worth your while by feeding you afterwards. How's that for a deal?" Mom said. Then she brought her hands to her chest and sighed. "Ah, it's so good to have my boys back under the same roof again."

Right about the time I thought my mom was going to cry, Beth walked in from the kitchen carrying a plate of those minty melts I could smell. Dressed in Uggs, black leggings, a fuzzy red sweater, and matching beanie, Beth looked beautiful and festive as usual. Her chestnut-colored hair bounced over her shoulders as she came into the room.

"Don't you look handsome today," Beth said as she kissed my cheek. She ran a hand down my navy-blue puffer vest as I eyed her plate of cookies.

"Just today? Thanks a lot, sis."

"Aww, you always look cute. But I don't know, there's something else going on that's different." She leaned back to take a look at my boots, hunter-green corduroy pants, and plaid shirt, then she grinned and said, "Maybe it's the hair."

That was her polite way of saying it definitely wasn't my outfit.

"Could be. It's a little longer than I usually wear it."

She nodded and then reached up to flick a piece that had fallen down over my forehead. "That has to be it. Looks good."

"So do you. But I think that's due to *this* wonderful accessory." I reached out and stole a melt off her plate, and she laughed.

"Mhmm," she said, and then offered one to Rick. "Better get one now before this one eats them all. You know how he is about anything chocolate and mint."

As I popped the melt into my mouth, I moaned as the flavor hit my taste buds. "So where is he? I heard you brought someone home this weekend."

Beth's cheeks flushed almost the same shade as her sweater, and Rick, being Rick, didn't let her get away with it.

"Ahh," Rick said as he wrapped an arm around our sister's shoulders. "Look at her getting all flustered about her new *boyfrieeend*."

Beth glanced behind her toward the tree, and then back to the two of us. "Would you keep your voices down? What are we, twelve?"

"No," I said as I stole another melt. "But we're your brothers and it's our job to give you shit. Where is he? Come on. You got him hiding in the kitchen?"

"Shut up," she said, and slapped me in the arm.

"Ow." I rubbed my abused bicep. "Mom, make her stop."

"Why would I do that?" Mom said. "You deserve it. Especially since Beth's gentleman friend is kindly trying to fix our tree."

I looked over Beth's head toward the tree that was covered in decorations from our childhood, and some new ones Mom had added this year. And as we moved closer, I noticed someone down on his knees at the back of the large spruce. He'd moved several of the wrapped gifts out of his way to get right in behind the tree, and just as we got there, my mom let go of my hand and walked over to the kneeling man.

"How are you going down there, dear?"

There was some rustling around and then the man's muffled reply: "Just fine, I think I almost—"

The tree lit up like a shining star, and my mom gasped. "Oh, you did it!"

Instant points for Beth's boyfriend right there. Whoever he

was, he'd just saved my mom's tree and therefore would likely be written into the family will.

Beth went over to him as he got to his feet, and then she took his hand in hers and brought him out from around the tree.

"Miles, I'd like you to meet my boyfriend, Sean," she said, and as the man beside her came into view, my stomach dropped and my heart sank. Like a deer in headlights, I froze, staring at the tall, dark-haired man who held my sister's hand.

Sean? That was what Beth called him, but that wasn't who stood in front of me, looking as shocked as I felt. Aiden was the name he'd given me last night when he'd kissed me under the mistletoe. And as fantasy and reality collided, I realized that *oh my God...*

I'd kissed my sister's boyfriend.

CHAPTER FOUR

AIDEN

OH SHIT.

THE two words played over and over in my head. But as I stood beside my latest client, Beth McAllister, I found myself face to face with the man I hadn't been able to stop thinking about since he'd vanished from my arms nearly twenty-four hours ago.

How in the world was it possible that I was standing opposite the cute, sexy nerd, whose lips had been sweeter than anything I'd ever tasted before, watching his face turn ashen? I knew I was the one to say our meeting was fate, but come on, this was just all kinds of messed up.

"*Miles?*" Beth said under her breath. "Don't just stand there, God. And here, I'd told Sean that my baby brother was the sweetest of us McAllisters."

I was so busy trying to sift through the information Beth had told me about her family, and work out how in the world I'd managed to miss something as monumental as her younger brother's name being Miles—as in Mistletoe Miles, my Miles, *her* Miles—that I missed him taking a step forward, and then promptly tripping on the lights I'd been fixing.

He stumbled forward, and before I knew it, Miles was back where he'd been hours earlier—in my arms.

"Oh shit," Miles said, and I couldn't help but chuckle because he'd just voiced my exact thoughts, unbeknownst to him. "I'm—" Miles cursed and clutched at my sweater as he righted himself, and Rick guffawed.

"You moron," Rick said. "Way to greet a guest. Don't worry about him, Sean, he's always been a klutz."

"That's okay," I said, as Miles let me go as though I was on fire —and not in a good way. "Things happen. Miles, is it?"

I held my hand out to him, wondering how exactly Miles was going to play this out, but it seemed he wasn't about to blow my cover just yet, because he slowly reached for my hand and said, "That's right. And you said your name was...Sean? Sean *what*, exactly?"

"Miles," Beth said, and slapped her brother in the arm. "Stop being so rude."

"No, it's okay," I said, and ran a hand up Beth's back, making sure to play my part to perfection—after all, that was what she was paying me for. But I also wanted Miles to know I hadn't lied to him last night about my name. "Sean Aiden Mahoney."

"Now if that's not a good Irish name, I don't know what is," Suzanne, Miles's mom, said, but I hadn't taken my eyes away from Miles, whose eyes were now darting back and forth between me and his sister.

"Anything else you want to know?" Beth asked Miles. "His age, social security number? Need a blood sample?"

Miles cocked his head to the side. "You're what, twenty-nine?"

I forced out a chuckle. "Nice guess."

"Yeah, it was. Do I win something for guessing right?"

"Why don't you have another cookie," Beth said, picking one up off the plate and shoving it into Miles's mouth for him.

His gaze left mine as he turned toward his sister, still chewing, and once he swallowed, he said, "So when did you two lovebirds meet?"

"Down, boy, down. I already grilled him," Rick said, throwing his arm around Miles's neck and dragging him away. "Who wants a drink?" he called out over his shoulder.

"Your father should be back soon with the rest of the supplies for mulled cider if you want to wait," Suzanne said, following after them with the tray of cookies she took out of Beth's hands.

From the kitchen, Rick let out a laugh. "No, we don't want to wait."

When we were left alone, Beth looked at me with apologetic eyes. "Sorry, I don't know what's gotten into Miles. He's usually so..."

"Antagonistic?"

"I was going to say friendly, but I can see why you'd think that."

"Maybe he's just tired. You said he had a long drive, right?"

"Yeah. I'm sure that's it." Beth looked over her shoulder to make sure we were still alone, and then said quietly, "Thank you again for being here. I already feel a load off."

"It's my pleasure."

A small smile crossed her lips. "And your job."

"No reason it can't be both." Along with frustration now that Miles had entered the picture to complicate things. How was I supposed to be in a house with him and his family for the long weekend *and* manage to fulfill my contract with Beth? It wasn't a situation I'd run into before, and it would be tricky to navigate, that was for sure. Especially when all I'd wanted to do when I saw Miles was repeat our kiss from the night before, but this time with no interruptions.

The front door burst open, and Jack, the McAllister patriarch, stepped inside, his arms weighed down with the dozens of grocery bags he carried. I hurried over to help take a load off at the same time Beth reached him.

"Hey, Dad," she said, then gave him a quick kiss on the cheek before heading to the kitchen to drop off the bags. I followed behind, but made sure to move to the opposite side of the counter to Miles and Rick, who both greeted their father with a hug and kiss to the cheek.

"I see everyone's met?" Jack said, looking between us all, and when his eyes landed on me, they narrowed a little. "Beth's been keeping this one a secret from us. Did you know about Sean here, Miles?"

Instead of answering, Miles raised his glass and downed whatever amber liquid was in it, and when he coughed, Rick slapped his back and said, "I told you to take it easy. You never drink whiskey."

Something I knew firsthand from the night before, and the reminder of that had Miles's eyes flying to mine. "I thought it would help warm me up. I'm feeling rather *cold*."

Yeah, the glare he was aiming my way was close to arctic in temperature, and then he put his glass on the kitchen island and turned toward his mom.

"I'm going to head upstairs and put my stuff in my room. When's dinner?"

"Oh, dear," Suzanne said, as she walked around the counter and placed a hand on Miles's arm. "I actually put Beth and Sean in your room, since it's the only one with a queen bed. I have you in the guestroom."

If I thought the stare before had been cold, well, the one that found me then was downright frigid.

"In my room?" Miles said. "Are you serious?"

"Miles," Jack said, clearly as shocked as everyone else by this stranger who'd inhabited their brother's body and made him a prickly version of himself. "I'm sure you'll survive. The bed in the guestroom is long enough for your legs. So how about you be a little more hospitable?"

Miles's jaw clenched, and he took a step back from the island. "You're right," he said as he walked past his brother, back toward the living room. "I'm just going to go and get my blanket for the guestroom. If these two...lovebirds aren't using that as well."

"No," Beth said. "I folded it up and put it on the chest at the end of the bed for you. I know that's your favorite."

Miles tried for a smile, but it looked strained as he raised a hand and then left the kitchen to head upstairs.

As he disappeared from sight, Jack looked at his wife across the kitchen island. "What's gotten into him?"

She shrugged. "I don't know. He's been acting peculiar since he got here. You don't think he's...on drugs, do you?"

"Oh, come on, Mom," Rick said. "This is Miles. He wouldn't even take a drag of a cigarette that one time I got busted and Dad punished us by making us all try it."

As the family continued to speculate over their brother and son's odd behavior, my eyes drifted to the living room, where I could hear footsteps punishing the stairs one at a time, and thought Miles was likely envisioning my face as he marched up them.

If only I could explain... "Hey, Beth?" I said in a lowered voice.

When she looked at me, I reminded myself I was here to help her this weekend. That was my job. But I'd be more effective if I wasn't thinking about what the man upstairs was stewing over.

"Do you mind if I run upstairs and try to smooth things out with your brother? I feel like we got off on the wrong foot, and, well, I'd just feel better if he didn't want to poison my eggnog."

Beth offered a kind smile. "You don't have to do that. He'll come around."

"I don't mind, really," I said, and tried not to sound too eager.

"Well," she said, and shrugged. "It might help. Plus, Miles isn't the type who'll punch you or anything. The worst he'll do is maybe slam a door in your face."

"Good to know. I'd just feel better if we could work out what's the matter and start over."

Lies. I knew exactly what was wrong, and I wouldn't be shocked if Miles suddenly became the type to punch someone in the face.

"Okay. You remember where the room is, right?"

I nodded, then squeezed her hand. "I won't be long. Promise."

As I walked through the living room, I looked up the staircase and wondered what exactly I was going to say to the man upstairs likely cursing my name—well, one of them, anyway—and knew I wasn't about to find out by standing down here.

It was time to go and face the music, and decide where this fickle little thing called fate was going to lead us now.

CHAPTER FIVE

MILES

HAT THE HELL is going on? ran through my head as I shut the door to my bedroom—oh, sorry, Beth and Sean/Aiden's bedroom—and slumped back against it. I felt as though I'd stepped into the Twilight Zone.

The entire drive up here today, I'd been mooning over the sexy stranger *Aiden* who'd kissed my brains out last night, only to walk into my childhood home and find him on the arm of my sister.

I mean, yeah, I'd had crushes on Beth's friends and boyfriends growing up, but never in a million years would I ever, and I repeat *ever*, want to kiss the same guy she was sleeping with. *Ew.* Just no. And now they were not only going to be kissing in front of me but sleeping in my damn bed.

This was officially a nightmare. A Christmas nightmare. All wrapped up in a big, shiny bow.

Shoving off the door, I walked to the chest at the end of the bed to grab the quilt my mom had made for me and tucked it under my arm, and just as I was about to turn around and get the hell out of the danger zone, I heard the door handle turn.

As if my feet knew something I didn't, they froze in place as the door was pushed open, and when Aiden—excuse me, *Sean*—

stepped through, I found I had no problem whatsoever speaking to this jackass. No. Unlike the night before, I had plenty to say, and none of it was nice.

"If you think for one minute I'm going to stand here and talk to you, you can forget it. So why don't you open that door and go back downstairs to your *girl*friend. You know, my sister."

A grimace tightened Aiden's lips, and as he squeezed the door-knob, I told myself to stay strong. *Do not feel bad because he feels like an ass. That's on him.* But when Aiden turned around as though he was going to do exactly what I'd said, I took a step forward and blurted out, "Why?"

With his back still facing me, I took in the broad shoulders under the grey-flecked sweater and how the color made his hair look like black silk, then I chastised myself for even noticing.

"Why were you at that party last night? Alone? Why did you..."

He turned around, and when his face came back into view, I clutched the quilt a little tighter.

"Kiss you?" Aiden said in the same voice I'd gone to sleep dreaming about the night before.

But then I shook my head and reminded myself that my sister likely went to bed hearing it in her ear, and yeah, that was enough to bring back my ire.

"I'm not doing this," I said, and as I walked forward, fully intending to storm by him, Aiden moved until he was in front of me.

"Miles..." he said, and reached out to touch my arm, but at the last second he must've thought better of it, because he dropped his hand back down by his side. "This is not what you think—"

"What I *think*? Please. Save your breath. I don't want to hear it."

As I went to shove by him, Aiden took hold of my arm and halted me. We were standing as close as we had been the night before, and as I glared into his dark eyes, I was reminded of how gorgeous he'd looked with snow clinging to his lashes.

"Don't leave like this," Aiden said. "Let me explain."

I licked my suddenly dry lips and tried not to focus on the feel of his fingers touching me. "What do you need to explain? You're my *sister's* boyfriend, Aiden. You're going to be sleeping with her in *my* bed." My incredulity all came roaring back at that, and suddenly I couldn't stop my rambling thoughts from spewing out of my mouth. "I mean, that's where I wanted you, sure. But not like this. I can't..." I yanked my arm out of his grasp. "I *won't* do this to her."

As I stepped around him and headed for the door, I took hold of the handle, but before I got it open, a large hand landed on the wood panel by my head.

"Move your hand," I said.

"Look at me." Aiden's voice was a low growl that stroked the back of my neck and made me powerless to do anything but obey. My hand left the handle, and it was as I turned around that I realized he had me backed up against the door. His other arm came up on the other side of me, caging me in, but instead of feeling claustrophobic or angry at his closeness, I felt my cock stir. *Traitor.*

My eyes locked on his mouth as his tongue came out to wet his lips, and God how I wanted to lean forward the few inches separating us and taste him. Last night wasn't enough, but it would have to be, because there was no way it could ever happen again—

"Oh, fuck it," was all I heard before Aiden's mouth was on mine. It took a few seconds for my brain to comprehend that he was kissing me, but that didn't stop my lips from parting so he could tangle his tongue with mine.

I groaned into his mouth as he cupped my neck and angled his head for a deeper kiss. It was hot and desperate, almost punishing, nothing like it'd been last night. No, last night had been sweet and romantic, but the way Aiden was kissing me now, it was like he had something to prove.

Aiden... No. *Sean.*

I pushed against his chest, breaking our lips apart. His pupils were blown, and I'd already felt the evidence of his arousal when our hips had been pressed against one another. His hand still cupped my neck, and I reached up to cover it with my own before pulling them both away.

Why did I do that? Kiss him? Why had I *let* him do that? And for the love of all that was holy, why did he have to taste so good?

"Miles—"

"No," I said, pushing against his chest again to keep him away. "You can't do that again. *We* can't."

"But—"

I pushed myself off the door, forcing him back. "If you try to kiss me again, I'm telling my sister. Don't think I won't. Leave me the hell alone."

And this time, before he could protest, I snatched the quilt I'd dropped from the floor and left without another word.

Once inside the safety of the guestroom, I locked the door and sat on the edge of the bed. My lips still tingled from the force of the kiss, and as I brought my fingers up to my mouth, I closed my eyes.

My mind whirled from everything that had happened in the last hour. I'd gone from being giddy over last night and spending the weekend with my family for Christmas, to the shock of my life seeing Aiden as my sister's boyfriend—God, would that ever sink in?—to two minutes ago when I'd *made out with said boyfriend.*

I dropped my head into my hands and groaned. *Great life decisions happening right now, Miles. Good job.* The last thing I'd ever want to do was hurt my sister, and I'd gone and kissed her boyfriend twice now. It was official: I was a jerk.

But I wouldn't let it happen again. Nope. I didn't understand what Aiden was playing at, but that wasn't on me. And if he kept on disrespecting Beth, I'd be the first to tell her.

Yes, good plan. Now I just had to work out how to get through the weekend with him.

CHAPTER SIX

AIDEN

*T*HE DOOR SLAMMED shut with a resounding *bang*, and I winced at the echo it left in its wake. I'd really screwed things up here. I'd come upstairs to try and smooth things out with Miles, and instead, I'd kissed him until I'd forgotten where I was.

Shit. This wasn't good. In fact, it was really, *really* bad. There was no way his family would've missed Miles's exit. Hell, I wouldn't have been surprised if his neighbors had heard the door rattle. But I wouldn't regret it. No. Sure, this was a monumental fuck-up of epic proportions, but once everything was explained, he'd understand. The key here was getting Miles to calm down enough to *let* me explain, which wouldn't happen if I kept kissing him.

I sighed, walked to the bed—Miles's bed—and sat down, thinking about all the things I'd do to him if I'd been allowed to pull him down onto it. And once again I was doing exactly what I shouldn't be doing: fantasizing about a client's brother.

This was a first for me, for sure. When I'd gotten into this gig three years ago, I'd thought it was an easy way to make some cash. My friends had always joked around that I was too smooth for my own good. Easygoing and personable, I'd never had a problem before fitting in with a client's group of friends or family. But then again, I'd never been in a situation quite like this either.

I'd purposely tailored my "business" to where I only took on female clients. It was less messy that way, considering I was gay, and I'd never have to worry about falling for any of them. But I'd never really considered what would happen if I fell for one of their *brothers*, because what was the likelihood of that happening?

Apparently, pretty damn likely. Which now made things really complicated.

Knock, knock, knock. "Sean?"

At the sound of Beth's hesitant voice, it was confirmed that the entire family had heard Miles's departure, and when she pushed open the door, she looked around the room as though double-checking no one else was in there with me.

"Just me," I said.

She came inside and shut the door, and once she was satisfied we were alone, she said, "Was that Miles we just heard?"

I gave a strained smile and nodded. "It seems your brother and I don't...umm, see eye to eye about playing nice."

"Really?" she said as she sat beside me. Her eyes were wide as saucers as she shook her head, and considering she didn't know the full story, I could see why she was so baffled that her apparently sweet brother had morphed into a total Grinch.

"I don't understand this at all." Beth pulled her beanie off her head and smoothed her hand over her waves. "Maybe he is on drugs? I mean, this is so unlike him. Miles is always so nice and welcoming. Rick's always been the overly protective one."

She glanced at the door, and then back to me. "I'm going to go and find him. He can't keep treating you like this. I don't care if this is just a ruse. You didn't sign up for this."

As she went to get to her feet, I reached out and halted her. "Wait." I could see the confusion in her eyes and tried to think of the best way to edge around the questions there. "I know this isn't ideal, but sometimes this is how it happens. Families...react differently to new people."

Beth frowned. "Not Miles. He *never* acts like this. He was always the one bringing home stray animals, new school friends, and asking poor George who collected money at the local mall over for Christmas dinner."

Of course he was.

"So this is... It's just not like him. He doesn't even know you. And he owes you an apology."

As she shot to her feet, I did too, and I knew I needed to either come up with something really convincing or just—"Beth, he does know me"—come clean.

Her forehead creased. "Miles knows you? How?"

I ran my hand through my hair and sighed. *Here we go.* "Look, I've never been in this situation before, but I feel the need to have total transparency here." When Beth nodded for me to go on, I said, "Miles and I have met a couple of times before, and the first thing you need to know about that is I go by a different name for my job. You know me as Sean, but he knows me as Aiden. And he...doesn't know what it is I do."

"Okaaay," she said. "So, is that why he's upset? He thinks you lied about your name?"

I wish it was just that. "No, that's not all."

Beth waited for me to keep going, but how did I tell her that I was developing feelings for her brother? That I wanted to get to know him better and—

"Sean? What are you not telling me?"

"Beth, I..." *Just say it. Rip off the Band-Aid.* "I like your brother."

The silence was deafening as she stared at me, confusion written all over her face.

"You *like* Miles?" she said, and then rubbed at her temples. "Are we talking *like* like, or—"

"I kissed him. Last night at a party." I wasn't about to tell her I did it again where she was standing a few minutes ago, because who needed those extra details when the truth was bad enough?

She gaped at me, her mouth opening and shutting like a fish. "Oh my God. You and *Miles*?" She paced for a moment before flopping down on the end of the bed. "Okay, this complicates things."

"Exactly," I said. "This isn't something I've ever encountered, and I won't let it affect my job with you, but I needed to let you know."

"Hang on. You said he doesn't know what you do...right?"

"Right."

"So he thinks you cheated on me with him? Oh my *God*."

"He threatened to tell you about it."

Beth let out a low chuckle. "Oh, Miles. I told you he's a good guy." Then she narrowed her eyes and smirked. "But apparently you already know that, huh?"

Shoving my hands in my pockets, I nodded. "I do."

"Wow. So, what do we do now?"

"Pray. We pray."

She laughed and fell back on the bed. "This is insane. I have to tell him the truth, or he's gonna make this weekend a living hell."

"What about your parents?"

"Miles won't say anything. They'll never know."

"You sure about that?"

"Positive. Although"—she lifted herself up to rest on her side —"we still need to keep this charade going, just for the weekend. They already love you, and it'll cause more drama my way if my parents find out. The whole point of bringing you here was to get them to lay off me, which is working like a charm."

"Agreed. I'll honor our contract. No need to worry about that."

"Oh no."

"What's the matter?"

"If you and Miles end up together, it's gonna look like I'm the one who turned you gay. I can't decide if that's worse than Spinsterville."

"I promise, you could never turn anyone gay."

"Aww. Sweet talker."

"Nah. The person you were with would already know they were gay."

Beth rolled her eyes, laughing as she got to her feet. "All right, I'm going to go talk to Miles. By the time you see him again, he'll be back to his sweet, charming self. I hope."

"Good luck. Maybe put on some combat gear first."

"Don't you worry, I can handle him." Beth paused as she got to the door and looked over her shoulder. "By the way, if you hurt Miles, just know I'm gonna kick your ass."

That was the second McAllister who'd threatened me in the last hour, and something told me it wouldn't be the last before the weekend was over.

After Beth winked at me and shut the door behind her, I blew out a breath. What was supposed to be a simple job had turned into something even I couldn't have anticipated. Would Miles understand? Would he help his sister out by staying quiet?

But even more than that, would he look me in the eyes the next time he saw me?

CHAPTER SEVEN

MILES

I WOKE THE next morning to the clanging of plates and muted chatter downstairs, signaling that the day had begun for my parents, and knew at some point this morning I would have to drag my ass downstairs and apologize to my mother.

Yesterday had been one shock after the other, and when Beth had tracked me down last night to explain what was really going on, I'd needed a moment—or a few hours—to process. I was still trying to recover from the whiplash I'd gotten from thinking the man of my dreams was actually Beth's man, and now it turned out that Aiden was actually...what? A date for hire?

What the hell was going on?

I wasn't sure if that was better or worse than if he'd just been her boyfriend. *Ugh.* I squeezed my eyes shut and told myself to stop overthinking things. Beth had assured me that Aiden was a good guy, but really? How good could he be? He dated people— and did God knows what else with them—for a living. This was just crazy.

Kicking back the covers, I got out of bed and grabbed my robe. Once it was fastened, I headed into the bathroom and washed up, and then I looked myself in the mirror and said, "You are an adult, and you need to act like one. Pull yourself together and go apologize to your mother."

I headed downstairs and heard the familiar sound of my sister's voice. I steeled myself against what I would encounter when I walked into the kitchen, and yep, sitting at the breakfast nook was Aiden.

He had on a pair of jeans and a cream cashmere sweater, and with his dark hair and eyes, and the perfect morning stubble along his jaw, he looked...amazing.

"There you are," Mom said, as she came around the island and held her arms out to me. "We missed you at dinner last night, but Beth explained you were feeling a little bit...tired."

I glanced at Beth, who was sitting beside Aiden, and she offered a half grin as she raised her mug of hot chocolate to her lips.

"Uh, yeah. I was, um...exhausted after the drive up here and just needed a good rest." I kissed my mom's temple. "I'm sorry for my behavior last night. I have no excuse."

"That's okay, baby, but I'm not the one you should be apologizing to."

As she looked at Aiden, I wished like hell the ground would open up and swallow me. God, I knew there was no way she would let this go. My mother had drilled good manners into all her children and prided herself on that, and right now I knew she was waiting for me to live up to her high standard.

I looked at Aiden, and when the corner of his mouth, that delicious damn mouth, crooked at the side, I gripped the edge of the kitchen island a little harder.

"I apologize for my rude behavior last night," I said, and my eyes flicked to my sister, who was biting her lip as though trying not to laugh—I'd kill her later for that. "I'm happy that Beth has found someone so...nice to bring home with her for the holidays."

Lame. Lame. *Lame.* Nice? Try hot, sexy, everything I wanted to bring home for the holidays wrapped up in cashmere.

Aiden inclined his head and said, "That's okay. I understand how stressful this time of year can be. Add in a stranger to the mix, and—"

"Oh, nonsense," Mom said. "That's what this time of the year is all about. Embracing our fellow man. Now don't you feel better, Miles? That you've kissed and made up?"

My eyes widened a fraction, and Beth coughed, but cool as can be, Aiden smirked and said, "I sure do."

"Good boys," Mom said, as she opened the fridge and pulled out a container of eggs. She set them on the counter, flipped open the lid, then frowned. "I thought I had more than this."

"Rick made spiked eggnog last night when you went to bed," Beth said.

"Well, that won't do. Miles, could you pop up to the shop and grab me a few more cartons?"

"Sure, Mom," I said.

"Actually, I have a few more things too. Let me write them down." She took a notepad out of a drawer and scribbled down some items, and as she tore the list and handed it to me, her eyes darted over to Aiden. "Perhaps since you didn't get a chance to get to know Sean last night, you could take him with you?"

What? "Uh, I don't think—"

"That's a great idea," Beth said, tossing a few more marshmallows into her mug. "Maybe grab a bag of Hershey's Kisses while you're out? I'm having a craving for some. Oh, but the ones with nuts."

If it were possible, my stare would've drilled a hole into my sister, but she smiled sweetly at me and sipped her drink.

"Why can't Rick do it?" I asked.

"Because Rick is out giving boxes of cookies to homeless shelters," Mom said, giving me a look that said not to give her any more lip.

"I'm good with going if you are," Aiden said, and as I swung my gaze to him, I didn't see any of the confident spark that had been there before. Instead, he seemed hesitant, like he was waiting to see what my reaction would be to him this morning. To be honest,

I didn't even know what I was thinking, but the idea of being alone with him made me a little nervous.

Relax. He's not kissing your sister. He's not really her boyfriend. It's not real.

"Let me just get dressed," I said, folding Mom's list and then heading back up the stairs. This wasn't a great idea, but I promised Beth I'd play nice and go along with her ruse, so I'd do that.

And hopefully not end up kissing Aiden again.

*T*EN MINUTES LATER, we were in my car, the heater on full blast as we sat in the driveway.

"It just takes a minute," I said, rubbing my gloved hands together to ward off the cold until the heat kicked in.

"No problem." Aiden stretched his long legs, and of course I couldn't help but look out of the corner of my eye. Why did he have to look so good? It wasn't right. Even bundled up in his jacket and scarf, he somehow looked like he'd just walked off a runway. Meanwhile, I'd only packed casual clothes, since obviously I'd had no idea I need to dress to impress.

Wait, no. I don't care about impressing anyone, and certainly not Aiden. Hell, he's seen me in a Grinch onesie. It can only go up from there.

Aiden cleared his throat. "You look really good in that red sweater."

My head jerked in his direction. "Uh-uh. Don't you start with me."

"I'm not starting anything."

"You are, and we should really keep things...platonic."

"A little late for that."

"We're starting over. You, me, a blank slate. One that doesn't involve kissing or...anything."

"And I can't tell you I like that red sweater on you?"

"You absolutely can't tell me that." The heater finally began to blow hot, and I backed out of the driveway and eased onto the road.

"Okay." Aiden fell silent for a moment, and I thought he'd actually heed my wishes. I should've known better, because a few seconds later, he said, "Then I'll just tell you I bet you look great *without* that red sweater on, too."

It was all I could do not to slam on the brakes and make him walk back to the house, *the smooth operator*.

Instead of responding—which was no doubt what he wanted—I flipped on the radio, which was still set on the holiday channel Holly and I had sung along to the day prior.

Aiden chuckled. "Ignoring me now? That won't work."

I clenched my jaw shut and hummed along with the music.

"Okay then. I can talk," Aiden said, shifting in his seat to face me. "Look, I know seeing me yesterday was a shock. It was for me too. And I wanted to tell you, but you didn't give me a chance."

"So instead of explaining, you decided to kiss me?"

A smile curled Aiden's mouth. "Got you to talk."

"Ugh." I zipped my lips shut and pretended to throw away the key.

"I didn't mean to kiss you. But I'd spent all day thinking about being with you at the party, and I couldn't help myself. Tell me you weren't thinking about me too."

He got the side-eye from me, though he wasn't wrong. But admitting that was *not* happening.

"When I saw you yesterday, standing there in front of me..." Aiden paused, and it was just long enough that I turned to see what he was doing, and our eyes met. "I knew there was nothing that was going to stop me from getting you alone and—"

"Kissing my brains out?" I blurted.

Aiden's lips twitched. "I was going to say explain."

I looked back at the road, wishing I'd held true to my original decision to keep my mouth shut, because I'd just embarrassed myself.

"But since you seem preoccupied with that, can I just point out I wasn't the only one in that bedroom last night?"

My mouth fell open and I tightened my hands around the

steering wheel. "That bedroom? You mean *my* bedroom. The one I thought you were sharing with my sister."

"Right," Aiden said as though this was the most normal conversation in the world. "Which you now know I'm not."

"So? Do you think that's going to make me just pull into a parking lot and jump you?"

Aiden let out a bark of laughter that made his irritatingly attractive face even more handsome. "That's probably too much to hope for, right?"

"Are you serious?"

"Dead serious, so if you find a place that looks good to you—"

"Aiden," I said, and then groaned. But damn the bastard, I could feel my lips curving into a grin. "You're impossible."

"And you're really fucking cute. Jesus, Miles."

I shifted in my seat, my cock really liking the way he'd said that. But I knew if we went down that road—or into that parking lot—there'd be no coming out of it. At least not for a few hours, anyway, and with the way I'd been behaving toward Aiden, my mom might think I took him somewhere to off him.

Best thing I could do for now was to distract him so he would stop looking at me in a way that made me want to launch myself across the console and kiss *his* brains out.

"So um...what made you go into this line of work, anyway? Actually, what the hell is your line of work? Are you an escort for hire? A gigolo? A gentleman caller? What is your actual title?"

Now that I'd asked the question that had been looping in my brain the most throughout the night, I had a million more questions to go with it, and before Aiden could answer, I was bombarding him with them.

"Is it just women? Or men too? Do you offer full service? Or is this just an 'I'll hold your hand' deal? And how does that work with your personal life? Isn't that awfully complicated?"

If I'd thought Aiden would get upset at my sudden inquisition, I was in for a surprise, because he chuckled good-naturedly.

"Let's see if I can put your...curiosity to rest a little, shall we?"

I narrowed my eyes, and he flashed a grin.

"I am *not* an escort or a gigolo. I sleep with who I want, when I want, and it's never for money. Nor is it ever about business."

Well, thank God for small mercies, because if he'd said Beth had asked him for that, I might've flung myself out of the car window.

"I work only with females, as there are fewer complications since, obviously, I'm gay."

"You 'work' with them?"

"Yes. I'm a relationship consultant."

I screwed my nose up as I looked at him again. "Um, what exactly are you consulting with Beth about? She's not *in* a relationship."

"Exactly. But your parents want her to be, and I'm here to help her deal with *that* relationship."

I scoffed. "So you're a boyfriend for hire, with a fancy name."

"Basically, yes."

"Wow. That's... I don't even know what that is."

"Helpful for people like your sister," Aiden said. "You should talk to her about it one day."

"Um, already did last night."

"No, not about her and me. Why she felt she had to bring me. You might be surprised."

As the two of us fell silent, and the holiday music continued to play, I thought back to something else I'd asked. "So, what about your own relationships? Doesn't your job make having one impossible?"

"I haven't had any issues in my past relationships, no. I know it may not seem like it to you now, but I'm always transparent with the person I choose to spend my time with. Then again, I've also never wanted to date one of my clients' family members."

Date? He wants to date me? "So what happens after this weekend?"

"With Beth and me?" When I nodded, he said, "The contract ends on Christmas at midnight."

"So you just...break up?"

"I don't think she'll tell your parents that news right away, but yeah, eventually. Unless there's another contract, we have no reason to see each other again."

"Huh."

"Did you have any other questions for me?"

"Not right now, but give me five minutes and I'm sure I will."

Aiden's deep laugh vibrated in the space between us. "I was going to ask Zack for your number when I got back in town."

"You were?" The stomach flipping was back, and I bit my lip. "Me too." As soon as the words were out of my mouth, I couldn't believe I'd said them.

"Really?" Aiden stretched his arm along the top of the driver's seat, his hand resting near the back of my head.

"I mean, I...thought you'd want me to," I said.

Aiden's smile grew. "I did. I still do."

"Yeah?"

"Definitely."

I had to pull my gaze away from his to concentrate on driving, but it was one of the harder things I'd had to do in my life.

"So about that parking lot..."

That made me chuckle. "The only parking lot we'll be seeing is the Whole Foods one."

"Can't blame a guy for trying. But I'll make an attempt to behave. For the weekend, anyway."

"Mhmm. Do you even know how to do that?"

"Apparently not around you. I've already broken several rules in my contract."

That shouldn't have made me smile like a loon, but for some reason, being the one person who'd affected Aiden like this was like some sort of Christmas miracle. One I wasn't going to dismiss so easily this time.

We both just had to keep our hands—and mouths—to ourselves this weekend. Three more days. That wouldn't be too difficult, right?

CHAPTER EIGHT

AIDEN

I GLANCED DOWN at the cards I held in my hand. I needed one more seven to give me a four of a kind. From across the table, Miles met my eyes briefly and then picked up the card that was moving clockwise around the coffee table. After a few seconds of consideration, he placed it facedown beside him and Suzanne picked it up. On it went until it got to me, and wouldn't you know it—a seven.

After switching out my cards, I waited until the attention was off me, and then I quietly reached for one of the spoons lined up in the middle of the table. The move didn't escape Miles, who'd been watching me out of the corner of his eye, and as he grabbed one of the spoons, utter chaos broke out, everyone screeching and fighting over the remaining cutlery.

I laid down my four of a kind and chuckled as Suzanne and Rick fought over the last spoon.

"I'm your mother, you should let me have it," Suzanne said, yanking on one end.

Rick jerked the spoon toward him. "I'm not *letting* you have anything. I grabbed it first."

"Did not."

"Did too."

Beth reached over and tickled Rick's ribs, and as he yelped, he lost his grip on the spoon, and Suzanne held it high over her head in victory.

"That's cheating," Rick cried.

"Oh, don't be a sore loser, honey. You've won several times already."

"If we're gonna be technical about it, Aid—Sean won this round," Miles said, gathering up the cards from everyone and giving them a good shuffle.

My lips tipped up. "Thank you, Miles." He didn't hold my gaze for long, just as he hadn't since we'd been alone in his car together yesterday. We were both behaving, both putting on an act for the benefit of Beth and his family, but it was one of the hardest things I'd done in my life.

With his wavy brown hair casually mussed from running his fingers through it, and wearing worn jeans and a white T-shirt with a red-and-blue plaid shirt unbuttoned over it, Miles was mouth-watering as hell. Seeing him in his parents' home, relaxed and joking around, only added to his appeal, and what was more, he seemed to have no idea how attractive he was. And it wasn't only his looks. It was his agreeable nature—well, now that he wasn't out to attack me anymore—and the easy way he laughed. From what I'd seen, he had a close-knit relationship with his siblings and parents, one I envied. It'd been so long since I'd seen my own family that I'd forgotten what it was like to be around people who cared about you, no matter what.

A furry body rubbed itself against my arm, and I looked down to see Lucifer pacing back and forth beside me. They'd all warned me that there was a demon cat that lived with them, and that he hated visitors and only came out when he was hungry, but I hadn't found that to be the case at all. Lucifer pawed at my lap, and I reached down to give him a head-to-tail rub, as Jack looked on in amazement.

"Seems like you've got the magic touch," he said, shaking his head. "Usually he scares off our guests."

"Hey, come here, little asshole," Rick said, reaching down to pet Lucifer, but when the cat hissed, baring his fangs, Rick jumped back. "Little asshole is right."

I laughed and scratched the spot behind Lucifer's ears, and as he began to purr, Miles's brows shot up.

"What did you do? Drug him with catnip?" he said.

I chuckled and continued to stroke Lucifer's soft hair. "Maybe I do just have the right touch?"

Miles smirked, and his eyes dropped to my hand, and I'd never wanted to read minds more than I did right then, because clearly he was right on track with my own thoughts. How would it feel if I was allowed to run my hands all over him?

"Sean? Babe?" Beth said, and when I looked her way, she grinned in a way that told me she hadn't missed what had just passed between myself and her younger brother. But she was doing her best to try and prevent the rest of the family from seeing too much. "Would you mind helping Miles get the dessert? I have a sudden craving for something sweet."

You and me both, I thought as Miles jumped to his feet, and I wondered if it was smart for me to go into a separate room with him right now, considering the thoughts running through my head.

I was busy trying to think of a good excuse to stay, when Miles shocked the hell out of me by saying, "Yeah, that'd be great if you don't mind. I mean, unless you want to stay here and stroke the cat..."

I wasn't sure if I was imagining the twinkle in his eye, but hell if I wasn't about to take him up on the offer he seemed to be issuing. As I got to my feet, I gave Lucifer a final pet and said, "Try not to claw Rick's face off," and then I followed Miles into the kitchen.

He went straight to the freezer, opening it up to get out a tub of ice cream, and I glanced over my shoulder to make sure everyone in the living room was occupied before standing beside the fridge.

"What's for dessert?" I asked.

Miles's eyes found mine, and he grinned. "I have no idea. But I couldn't stand sitting across from you any longer without looking at you the way I really want to, so this seemed like a good way to get you alone."

I chuckled as he stood with the freezer door open, blocking our faces in case anyone walked in on us. "To get me alone, huh? Technically, your entire family is sitting in the other room."

"Yeah. But at least no one's here watching my every move."

Oh, I liked the sound of that. "So...how do you want to look at me, Miles?"

Miles took in a shaky breath, and as he ran his eyes down over me, he bit his bottom lip and—

"Okay, you need to stop looking at me like you want to."

Miles laughed as he shut the freezer door, and then walked to the kitchen island. As I sidled up beside him, he said, "Can you get out the spoons and bowls? Do you remember where they are?"

I nodded and grabbed them for him, and when I came back, Miles opened up the ice cream and grabbed the scooper.

As he began piling scoops into each bowl, Miles said under his breath, "You smell really good, by the way. Do you know that? Like, I want to crawl in your lap good."

"Jesus, Miles," I said, as I kept my eyes on the family laughing around the coffee table in the next room. "What happened to your rule about behaving ourselves until the weekend was over?"

Miles stopped scooping and looked at me, and his mischievous grin was downright adorable. "I'm behaving. I'm not *touching* you, am I?"

"If you were touching me, we'd be in a lot of trouble."

The curious spark that lit his eyes told me that was the exact wrong thing to say, and when he lowered his voice and said, "What kind of trouble?" I couldn't stop the rumble of laughter that left my throat.

"If we weren't surrounded by your *entire* family what would be the first thing you'd want me to do to you?"

Miles froze, and his hand tightened around the handle of the scoop.

"So are we playing charades?" I said. "Want me to guess what that handle is representing?"

Miles picked up the scoop and ran his tongue along the back of the metal, and I had to grip the island to stop myself from taking hold of him and taking his now extra-sweet lips with mine.

"Are you trying to drive me crazy?" I said, shaking my head.

Miles gave a flirty shrug. "Maybe. You kind of deserve it, don't you think?"

Ahh, so that was what this was about. Miles had decided to give a little payback for my surprise arrival. "If this is your way of punishing me, I'm a fan. But you still didn't answer me. What's the first thing you'd want me to do to you?"

Miles ran his eyes down to my fingers on the granite counter, and then reached out to trace the back of my hand. My cock reacted to the touch as though his fingers had just stroked it, and standing as close as we were, I could see his blue eyes darken. Then he swallowed, and I braced myself for whatever was about to come out of his delectable mouth.

"I'd want you to put your hand—"

There was a crash and a screech. "Lucifer!"

Suzanne's shout jolted me out of the fantasy I was having of putting my hands anywhere on Miles, and before I could comprehend what was going on, a flash of black wrapped in gold streaked across the kitchen floor and bounded up onto the counter—a trail of tinsel and glitter in his wake.

"You get down off the counter right now, you little hellion!" Miles's mom shouted as she raced in after the cat.

Miles blinked once, twice, and then turned around just in time to see Lucifer land a front paw in the tub of ice cream as he scrambled across the counter.

"Lucifer, get down!" Miles shouted as he swatted at him, which only made the cat more frantic. As Lucifer's paw sank into the ice cream like a foot in quicksand, he grabbed for whatever he could nearby to try and pull himself free—which just so happened to be the bowls we'd been filling.

One by one, the bowls went flying, smashing to smithereens on the slate floor, and as the entire McAllister family chased after the cat, Lucifer took a flying leap for freedom off the end of the counter, the tinsel twisting around the tub and flinging it across the space, where it smashed into the stainless-steel fridge.

Each family member took a side, running around the island trying to capture the beast before he got ice cream and glitter all over the house, but every time someone got close, the little furball managed to dodge them and make a break for it.

"You little shithead," Jack said as he closed in on the cat, who was now shaking his paw, trying to get the ice cream off, but as Jack reached down to grab him, Lucifer hissed and sidestepped with a quick pounce to the left.

The mayhem went on for a good ten minutes. How many humans did it take to wrangle a demon cat? Apparently a few more than the McAllisters had up their sleeves, but then, finally, little Lucifer came to a stop by my feet.

I looked down at the furball who was currently matted with the sticky cream, and as he glanced up at me, the look in his eyes was *yeah, just try it, pal.* But then, as if the mess on his paw sidetracked him, he shook it again and brought it up to his mouth. He licked at it once, twice and then...oh yeah, that seemed like a great idea.

"Wait," I said to everyone who was still in a mad rush. "Stop for a second."

As they all froze, I looked at Beth, who was standing by the sink.

"Very slowly, pass me the dishtowel."

Beth inched her hand over to one, keeping her eyes on the still-licking Lucifer, and once she handed it over, I spread the towel wide and knelt beside the cat. He stopped licking long enough to look up at me and let out a loud meow.

"I know, buddy. Tastes good, huh?" When he meowed again, I

kept my hands steady and wrapped him up in the towel. To my surprise, he didn't put up a fight and let me pick him up. "There we go. Let's get you unraveled and then we'll see about getting the ice cream off."

As Lucifer went back to licking his paws, I looked up to see the entire McAllister family gaping at us.

"I think you should take him home with you. Consider it an early Christmas present," Jack said, but Suzanne playfully smacked him in the stomach.

"That was my mother's cat, and whether we like it or not, we're his forever home."

Jack groaned. "But he hates us. He loves Sean."

"I'm not listening," Suzanne said, plugging her ears as she headed to the sink to wash off the spewed ice cream.

"Well, since Sean's got this under control, I'm gonna head out," Rick said, grabbing his keys.

"Where are you off to so late?" Suzanne asked.

"Oh, I thought I told you. I'm meeting the guys out for pool."

"Pool. That sounds fun," Beth said, raising an eyebrow. "Can we come too?"

Rick scratched the back of his neck. "Uh, no. Guys' night and all."

"Mhmm. Right." Beth went back to wiping up the splatters of ice cream littering what seemed like every surface of the kitchen as Rick headed out, and I gently untangled the tinsel from Lucifer's body.

"Seems like you really do have the magic touch with pussy... cats," Miles said in a low voice only I could hear as he sidled up beside me. "Should I be worried about that?"

I snorted out a laugh, startling Lucifer. "Jealous?"

"Maybe a little. Lucifer's seen more action than I have the past couple of days."

Glancing up to see where the rest of the McAllisters were, I said under my breath, "We can remedy that whenever you like."

"Oh yeah? I may have a handle you can squeeze—"

"Miles!"

We both jumped, a guilty expression on Miles's face, as Suzanne stood a few feet away, her hands on her hips.

He cleared his throat. "Uh, yes, Mom?"

She narrowed her eyes and looked between the two of us, and my stomach dropped. Shit, had she heard us? This was not good—

"Are you going to help clean up, or are you going to antagonize Lucifer while Sean's trying to keep him calm?" she said.

Miles glanced at me, his creased forehead smoothing out, and then he backed away and took the broom Beth held out to him.

Flirting with Miles had taken an interesting turn tonight, and it thrilled something deep inside that had lain dormant for far too long. When had I last been this enamored with anyone? Miles was a breath of fresh air, one I craved more with every minute I spent with him. I knew we were supposed to behave this weekend, until the contract was over, but how was I supposed to go that long without getting my hands on him?

Truth? I didn't think I could.

CHAPTER NINE

MILES

I GLANCED AT the digital clock on the side table and groaned when I saw that it had just turned one thirty. *Great.* I wasn't having any luck falling asleep tonight, and there was nothing I hated more than lying in bed staring at the ceiling. But I knew the exact reason for my insomnia, and he happened to be sleeping four doors away on the floor of my childhood bedroom.

I grabbed the quilt and pulled it up under my chin as I rolled onto my side and wondered if Aiden was having as hard a time sleeping as I was—okay, maybe a *hard* time was the wrong way to phrase it. An accurate one, but not the one I needed to be thinking about right now.

After the disaster with Lucifer after game time, and cleaning the mess he'd left in his wake, I would've thought my eyes would shut the second my head hit the pillow. But all I could think about was the way Aiden had looked sitting at the coffee table with my family playing cards, the way he'd smiled and flirted with me in the kitchen, and the delicious way the man smelled...

Yeah, that wasn't going to help me get any rest.

I shut my eyes, willing sleep to find me, but the longer I lay there, the more elusive it became. Grumbling, I rolled to my back and gave up entirely. I stared at the fan above my head and thought back over everything that had happened since I'd arrived home. Now that I was over the shock of Aiden being here, and why, I had to admit I'd taken a step back to really examine why Beth had felt the need to "hire" him in the first place.

Sure, we all teased her about when she was going to get married and give my parents grandchildren, and mom was always on about how she just wanted Beth happy. But was it really fair to think that the only version of happiness for a woman in her thirties was married with children?

I already knew the answer to that: no.

Just like it wasn't fair to think I'd find a nice young girl and settle down. Everyone's version of happiness was different, and it hadn't even occurred to me how much it bothered Beth when we ribbed her about it. But it must if she'd gone to such lengths to avoid it this year.

I made a promise to myself to talk to her about it tomorrow, and I was about to try again for some kind of shuteye when I heard the handle of the guestroom turn. I propped myself up on my forearms to see who it was or what was wrong, and when the moonlight caught on Aiden's face, my eyes widened.

Oh my God. What is he doing here? But when he shut the door and I heard the distinct sound of the lock clicking into place, I decided I didn't really care.

"Miles?" he whispered, and when he took a step forward, my heart began to pound.

"You better be glad it's me," I said, and couldn't stop the ridiculous grin I knew was on my face. A low chuckle made its way through the dark and wrapped around me, as Aiden stopped at the foot of my bed. "How would you have explained that to Rick...or my father?"

"Lucky for me, I found the right bed with exactly who I wanted in it."

If it was possible, my grin became even wider, and while I knew we'd made a promise to behave this weekend, there was no way I was about to send him out the door without finding out the reason he'd been looking for me.

"And now that you found me?"

Aiden walked around the bed, and as he came closer, my eyes tracked every step he took.

"Now that I've found you," Aiden said, "I've decided to see how quiet you can be." He lifted the sheets up and slid in beside me. The bed in the guestroom was only a full size, so he had to scoot in close so he wouldn't fall off the mattress.

Umm, I wasn't complaining. At all.

Pushing myself up on my elbow, I shook my head. "You're crazy."

"Maybe. Is this okay?"

Was it okay? It was my fantasy come to life, though when I'd imagined Aiden in my bed, that bed wasn't in the guestroom of my parents' house. I wasn't about to be picky, though.

"It's more than okay," I whispered, settling my head in my hand to match Aiden's pose only inches from me. He wore a thin blue T-shirt and grey pajama pants, and it occurred to me that I wasn't wearing nearly that much. My chest was bare, and I had on only a pair of boxers.

As if he knew what I was thinking, Aiden pushed the covers down to my waist, devouring me with his eyes. I should've felt self-conscious, even though the room was dark except for the sliver of moonlight creeping in between the drawn curtains, but...I didn't. I liked the way he was looking at me, and the way his hand came up to trail lightly from my shoulder to my hip, leaving goosebumps on my skin.

"That feels good," I said, watching him as his fingers trailed back up my arm and moved to my chest. My body trembled. I couldn't help it. Just looking at Aiden caused a physical reaction I couldn't explain. Even though in the back of my head, I knew we shouldn't be doing this here, I couldn't find the will to stop and make him leave. Not when I wanted to touch him too.

When his fingers reached the place over my heart, I caught his wrist, and he stopped to look up at me.

"This is hardly fair," I said.

Aiden quirked a brow. "Is there something you want, Miles?"

"Yes. I want your shirt off."

With a wicked grin, he pulled away and removed his shirt, tossing it onto the floor.

Good God. Are you kidding me?

Aiden's body was nothing but defined muscles beneath smooth skin, not an ounce of fat anywhere. If he'd come in looking like that, I would've hidden under the damn covers.

"Wow," I said, as he scooted closer, and then his lips came down to press softly against my shoulder.

When he lifted his head, he smiled. "My thoughts exactly."

Mere inches separated us, but it still wasn't close enough. I ran my fingers over the stubble covering his jaw and remembered how it felt when he'd kissed me before. I needed those lips on mine again, and this time, I wouldn't wait for him to make the first move.

Before I could talk myself out of starting something I didn't know if we could finish, I brought his face to mine and crushed our lips together, both of us moaning at the initial contact.

Damn, he tasted as good as he looked and felt even better. I didn't waste any time diving into his mouth, and he seemed just as greedy, wrapping his hand around the back of my neck to pull me closer. But I quickly realized that wasn't close enough, because Aiden's arm wound around my waist, hauling me on top of him. His arousal pressed into my hip, and I was sure mine was just as obvious, especially since thin boxers were all I wore.

"God, Miles," he murmured against my lips, as he reached down inside my boxers to grab my ass with both hands, squeezing and then bucking his hips up, creating a delicious friction between us that had my eyes rolling in the back of my head. "You feel so perfect."

"Shh," I said, then covered his mouth again with my own, even though I wanted to hear more of his words. We didn't need anyone waking up to discover him missing from Beth's bed. "Quiet, remember."

"Hmm," Aiden said against my lips. "In that case, you better shut me up."

I grinned against his lips, and when he spread his legs and put his feet on the mattress so I could nestle down between them, I squeezed my eyes shut and burrowed my face into the crook of his shoulder.

Aiden rolled his body up against mine, and his new position added a forceful momentum that had a throaty moan leaving my lips, and when his fingers crept between my ass cheeks, I shuddered.

"Oh God," I said by his ear.

"Uh-uh. *Quiet*, Miles..."

I pushed myself up and planted a hand by either side of his head, and as I looked down at him, I bit into my lip and ground my erection over the top of his. Aiden's fingers dug into my naked flesh, and he shoved his head back into the pillow, and damn, he looked sexy. So sexy I couldn't seem to keep my hips from moving.

I grabbed hold of the pillow on either side of Aiden's dark hair and began to thrust over the top of him. Aiden's hands molded to my body, and he growled low in his throat, and I couldn't help but wonder how it would be when we could actually make noise—because I planned to make a lot of it next time with him.

And yes, there would be a next time if I had any say in the matter.

"Miles..." Aiden said, and this time my name sounded like a wish, which was fitting, since he had been mine. "You look and feel like a dream."

I let go of one side of the pillow and trailed my fingers down the side of his face, and then I cupped his jaw and took his mouth with mine, wanting to taste his lips, wanting to feel his body tremble against mine, wanting to swallow the sound of his groans as I memorized every single thing about the way he was moving beneath me.

As our kiss intensified, so did the movement under the sheets, and when the pleasure became too overwhelming, the emotions too much to bear, my toes curled and I felt Aiden's body tense beneath mine.

I tore my mouth from his to bury my face in his neck, knowing there was no way I would be able to keep quiet through such an overpowering release, and when he craned up to sink his teeth into my shoulder, I knew he was thinking the same thing.

The muffled groan and the way his body vibrated against mine sent me over the edge, and not a second after, I was right there with him, trembling in his arms, blissed out in a way I'd never been in my life.

Aiden let me sink down, boneless, into his body and wrapped his arms around me as we struggled to keep our heavy breathing down in the silent aftermath.

Had I just... Had we... I couldn't even think straight. My nose grazed against the sensitive spot beneath his ear, and I inhaled his scent deep into my lungs, committing it to memory along with what we'd just done. If it never happened again, I'd still die a happy man, but something told me this wasn't the end of Aiden and me, but the beginning.

CHAPTER TEN

AIDEN

"THIS HAS TO be the best sweet potato casserole I've ever had," I said, as I scooped another helping onto my plate. Did I need it? Hell no. But I couldn't help myself when it came to Suzanne McAllister's cooking. The last couple of days I'd probably packed on ten pounds, but it was worth it.

"I'm so glad you think so." Suzanne handed me the basket of rolls. She'd made a honey walnut butter to go with them, and I had no doubt that with the amount of rolls we'd all devoured, we'd be in a carb coma after lunch.

"Sean, we've sure enjoyed having you join us this weekend," Jack said, as I passed the basket his way. "I hope this means we'll get to see a lot more of you in the future."

Miles's leg brushed against mine under the table, and it was all I could do not to look his way. Beside me, I could feel Beth's gaze, and I gave her a small smile before turning to Jack.

"I've had a wonderful time. I appreciate you opening your home to me." Then I winked at Suzanne. "And feeding me so well."

"Oh, you just come see us anytime, you hear?" she said, clasping her hands under her chin. "We're just so glad our Beth has finally found someone, and such a sweet, handsome man, too. You two would give us gorgeous grandbabies."

Beth choked on her water. "Mom!"

"What?" Suzanne said. "I'm sure you two have talked about the future. I mean, it doesn't have to be tomorrow, but the clock *is* ticking, dear."

"Oh my God." Beth groaned and put her head in her hands. "I'm not *that* old. It's not like there's an expiration date."

"But there is—"

"Not anymore. Women have kids when they're fifty now—"

"*Fifty?* That's preposterous."

"It's called a different time and medical advancements," Beth said, her face flushed.

Miles shook his head. "I'm glad I don't have ovaries."

"Just because you can't reproduce doesn't mean I don't expect a few kiddos out of you, too," Suzanne said, waving her fork in his direction.

"Uh, maybe Rick can help you out there," Miles said.

Rick shrugged and stabbed a forkful of turkey. "Yeah, why not. Can't let the super sperm go to waste."

"Rick! You can't just say super sperm at the table," Beth sputtered.

Miles screwed up his nose. "I don't think you're supposed to say super sperm *ever*."

"Can we please talk about something else not related to babies or...anything that makes babies," Beth said, pushing her plate away.

"All right, all right," Jack said, holding his hand up. "Sean, why don't you tell us more about your family."

I would've rather kept talking about babies. Thinking of my family, especially around the holidays, chafed, and there was no way to explain why to Jack or anyone in the family, except Miles and even Beth. I couldn't exactly come out and tell them my family had shunned me for being gay, something I'd hidden from them for years because I'd expected their reaction and hadn't wanted to be left all alone just yet.

71

"I, uh..." I tugged at the collar of my shirt. "I don't have a family to speak of."

"What?" Suzanne gasped and clutched her necklace. "What do you mean you don't have a family?"

"Just that. There's a...fundamental disagreement." I met Miles's eyes then, and his were full of understanding and sorrow. His leg brushed against mine again, and it eased the tension in my chest.

"Oh, honey." Suzanne reached over to lay her hand on my arm. "I'm so sorry, but know you're always welcome here."

"That's right," Jack said, giving me a compassionate smile as Beth rubbed my back.

The crazy thing was that, under any other circumstances, I knew this family would accept me. That just seemed to be the kind of people they were. But how would they feel knowing I'd been lying about who I was?

"I appreciate that," I said, suddenly feeling as though I'd lost out on a good thing. "Thank you."

"Of course. You're helpful with Christmas lights, wrangling cats, and not hard on the eyes either. Beth has snagged herself an absolute gem," Suzanne said with a wink, and Beth groaned, but I chuckled. I'd never felt more comfortable, or welcome, than I did here in this house, and wasn't that something?

"Okay, can we move along from this topic?" Beth said. "Or Sean will never want to come back."

I reached for my glass of wine, and as I took a sip, Suzanne said, "Fair enough," and looked across the table to her youngest, who was piling some turkey and stuffing onto his fork. "What about you, young man?" When Miles realized she was talking to him, he looked at his mother. "Are you seeing anyone special we should know about?"

I wasn't sure if it was my imagination—or my brain slowing down time and zooming in on the man across from me—but I was positive I saw Miles's fingers tighten around his fork at the same time his eyes widened. *Oh my God. Is he choking?*

When no words left Miles—no sound at all, actually—Rick smacked him on the back.

"You okay, bro?" he asked.

When Miles's eyes inadvertently caught on mine, it was my turn to rub my leg up against his. The poor guy looked like a deer in caught in headlights.

When he still said nothing, I arched an eyebrow at him, and it was as though he finally got the jolt—or rub—he needed to find his voice.

"I'm fine," Miles told his brother, and then looked at Suzanne. "I've actually just met someone."

Holy shit. I had not expected him to say that.

"You did?" Suzanne said, lowering her fork.

"Good for you, man," Rick said around a mouthful as Miles looked at me and Beth and said, "I did."

I tried my hardest not to picture Miles the way he'd looked last night stretched out on top of me, but it was close to impossible with our legs connected beneath the table and his blue eyes all but sparkling at me. But, luckily for us, Beth was more than happy to save our foolish asses, since we seemed incapable at that particular moment.

"Well I wish you'd brought him home with you, so we could've talked about something *new* this year."

Miles's eyes shifted to his sister, and beneath the mischievous light, a hint of sympathy crept through. "I told you, I just met him. And I'm sure he had other plans anyway."

"You can't leave it at that," Suzanne said. "What's his name? What's he do? Oh, what's he look like?"

Miles's eyes flicked to mine ever so briefly then, before he turned back to his mom and shrugged.

"I told you, I just met him."

"What? So you don't even know his *name*?" Rick said, his fork clanging down on the plate. "And here I thought you were the romantic out of all of us."

73

"I am," Miles said, then put the mouthful of food between his lips and chewed. He gave a carefree shrug and added, "I've decided to leave it to fate. If he's meant to be in my life, then I'm sure he'll turn up again...right?"

"Aww," Suzanne said. "That is romantic. But you can at least tell us what he looks like."

Miles reached for his glass of wine. "Perfect."

"Oh *God*." Rick moaned. "Someone get the guy a bib. I think he's about to start drooling."

As the family continued to talk all around us, I did my best to pay attention and contribute, but if someone had asked me later what they'd talked about after that, I would've had a hard time remembering, because all I could see and hear were Miles's words running on a loop in my head.

"Well, I don't know about all of you, but I'm stuffed," Jack said as he sat back in his chair and rubbed his full belly.

"Me too," Beth agreed. "It was delicious as usual, Mom."

"Thank you," Suzanne said with a grin. "I think we should all move to the living room around the fireplace, what do you think? Warm up, maybe even make some hot chocolate?"

"Great idea," Miles said, as he got to his feet and set her plate on top of his. Then he leaned in and kissed her on the cheek. "Great meal, Mom."

As the rest of us pitched in with the cleanup, Suzanne and Jack put on some classical Christmas music and settled into their recliners in the living room, while Miles did his best to touch me at every possible turn, arms grazing each other as we both reached for the mashed potato bowl, or "accidentally" bumping into each other at the sink. Those not-so-innocent touches, along with the memories of last night and what he'd just said at the table, lit a fire in my veins.

It wouldn't take much more for me to fall completely head over heels for Miles McAllister. Trying to hold myself back from him this weekend had been difficult, when all I wanted was to know anything and everything about him. I wouldn't mind if those Q&A

sessions were interrupted with lots of kissing, but it was more than just being physically attracted to Miles. I *liked* him. Really liked him, something that completely knocked me off my feet. And as much as I was enjoying the weekend with his family, I couldn't wait to get back to the city and finally spend some one-on-one time together to see where this thing could go.

We finished cleaning up and all headed into the living room, where Jack knelt in front of the fireplace, trying to get it going.

"I'm gonna need more wood for this to last a while," he said, and when he went to stand up, Miles put his hand on his dad's shoulder.

"Rick and I can do it," Miles said, and Rick nodded as his cell phone went off. He glanced down at the screen and swallowed.

"Actually, I need to take this, so give me a few," Rick said.

I stood up from the couch with Beth. "Take your time. I'll help Miles."

Rick nodded. "Thanks, man." He headed upstairs to take the call, while I followed Miles out the back door.

The snow had been falling steadily over the weekend, forcing us to trudge through the white mounds that came up to mid-shin. Jack kept a covered wood pile beside his shed, and as we reached it, I looked over my shoulder at the house and then reached for Miles's wrist. He turned around to face me, and I dropped my hold on him.

Miles's breath came out in white puffs, but as I stood there opposite him, all I felt was warmth from the expression in his eyes. He was looking at me the same way he had the night of Zack's party under the mistletoe, and it made me feel like I'd won some kind of prize.

"You caught me by surprise in there," I said, as I took a step toward him.

"Did I?"

I grinned at his coy act, falling even more under this sweet spell of his. "Yes, you did. But I think you already know that."

Miles brought his gloved hand up between us and held his thumb and forefinger a couple of inches apart. "Maybe a little."

"Mhmm." I glanced over my shoulder to make sure we were still alone, and when the coast remained clear, I took a step closer.

"I hope you don't mind," Miles said, but I was certain he knew I didn't mind in the slightest.

"The only thing I mind is that I wasn't sitting beside you when you said it."

Miles bit his lower lip, and when he moved even closer, it took everything in me to keep my hands jammed into my pockets.

"I think you might like me, Sean Aiden Mahoney."

"Miles..." I said, his name leaving my lips before I could help myself.

"Mmm, say that again," Miles said, and shut his eyes.

"Miles," I said, and before I thought twice about it, I raised my hand and ran my fingers down his cheek. "I know I said before that I believe in fate. But you...you are more than I ever could've hoped for."

Miles's eyes fluttered open, and as he turned his cheek into my palm, the light snow flurries that had begun to fall again caught on his long lashes.

Damn, he's beautiful. "I feel like I've fallen into a winter dream, one I don't ever want to wake up from."

"Aiden..." Miles whispered, and moved the final step forward until he had to tilt his head up to look at me, and his lips were so close and so perfect that I found myself lowering my head to brush mine against them.

The second we connected, I felt as though I was once again swept up in the magic that was Miles. The feeling that there was so much more going on here than just the physical; it'd been that way from the second we'd met and touched, that instant connection, and I never wanted it to end.

Miles's hands came up between us to take hold of my sweater, and as they tightened and he moved up to his toes, lost in the moment, I closed my eyes and finally let the idea of *us* take hold of me.

Completely absorbed in our little snow-globe moment, neither of us heard the back door open, or the heavy footsteps trudging through the snow. No, it wasn't until Rick's voice pierced the air that we jerked away from each other.

"What the hell do you think you're doing?"

CHAPTER ELEVEN

MILES

*W*HAT THE HELL *do you think you're doing?* Nothing could've brought reality crashing back down quicker than my brother's words. Aiden and I had pulled away from each other, but the damage was done. I could see Rick over Aiden's shoulder, a mix of confusion and rage on his face as he looked between the two of us.

I needed to defuse the situation, and I had to do it carefully. I knew all too well how hotheaded my brother could be when he was upset, but once I explained, he'd understand. I hoped.

Stepping away from Aiden, I lifted my hand as if to calm a wild animal. "Just give me five minutes. I'll tell you everything—"

"You'll tell me how you were just making out with our sister's *boyfriend?* What the hell, Miles? What are you doing?"

"Look, I know what it looks like, and yes, he's technically Beth's boyfriend—"

"*Technically?*" Rick said. "You've got a lot of fucking nerve doing this, and under Beth's nose?" He shook his head, and then his eyes narrowed on Aiden. "And you..."

Instinctively, I stepped in front of Aiden. "Leave him out of this. It's my fault."

"Like hell it is," Rick said, starting forward.

I held my hands out to my sides and forced Aiden to back up with me, because Rick wasn't stopping.

"Rick, it's just pretend," I said. "He's not really her boyfriend, he's—"

"You'd better fucking run, buddy," Rick said, not even listening to anything I said, his eyes stuck on the man behind me as his nostrils flared and he moved into a charging position.

Oh shit.

"Uh, Aiden?" I said.

"Yeah?"

At that moment, Rick charged forward, and I yelled, "Run!"

"What?" Aiden said, but when he realized Rick was seriously about to mow him down, he turned and ran. The snow being a couple feet high in spots didn't help his getaway, and he had to practically high-knee-it away.

Rick tore past me, and I flung myself his way, wrapping my arms around him from behind to try to stop him, but he was too muscular for me to get a good hold on, and my arms slipped. I grabbed for the only thing I could, which happened to be the tail of his shirt, and as he chased after Aiden, I bumped along the snow after him like I was nothing more than a bouncing ball.

"Rick," I yelled, panting. "This is stupid. Just stop."

"Leave it, Miles," he growled as we got closer to Aiden. "This guy thinks he can just mess with my sister *and* my brother? Not on my watch."

Aiden made it to the high gate and struggled to wrench it open, but the snow was too tall, and he searched around for something to help or somewhere to go.

"Go inside," I called out, knowing if Rick got any closer, Aiden's handsome face was done for.

"Get off me," Rick said, throwing me off into the snow, and then he dove forward, catching Aiden's sweater and knocking him off balance. But Aiden was able to grasp the backdoor handle, and it stopped him from falling into the snow, where my brother would no doubt attempt to bury him.

As Aiden disappeared inside the house, I pushed Rick from behind, catching him by surprise, and as he face-planted into the snow, I shouted out in victory.

"Take that, you bully," I said, starting for the house. "And don't say a word about this to Mom and Dad."

Rick's hand shot out to grab my ankle, and as I tried to kick him off, he grabbed my other leg, and I fell down beside him, snow instantly seeping through my clothes. He laughed as he left me there, flinging open the back door and running inside, and I quickly scrambled through the cold, wet stuff after him.

Aiden was standing in the living room with Beth, who had a puzzled look on her face, and then he did a double take when he saw Rick barreling down the hall, with me running after him.

"Gotta go," Aiden said, taking off for the front door.

"What's going on?" Beth said, her eyes widening when she saw Rick and me, and behind her, my parents both got to their feet.

"Rick?" my mom said, a crease forming between her brows. "Miles?"

Rick didn't stop, though, whizzing past them all and out onto the front lawn, where Aiden had rolled a couple of snowballs and lobbed them his way in an attempt to get him to stop.

Or anger the bull more, as it were.

When one hit Rick smack in the face, he drew to a stop and pointed at Aiden across the yard. "You're dead, Mahoney. You hear me? *Dead.*"

"Rick, stop," I said, standing in front of him to block his path yet again. "This is stupid. You don't even know what's going on."

"Oh, I saw what's goin' on, little brother," he said, patting me on the shoulder. "And don't worry—you're next."

A warrior cry sounded, and from out of nowhere, Beth ran toward Rick and jumped onto his back.

"What are you doing?" Rick yelped. "Get off. Don't you see I'm defending your honor?"

"My honor? By attacking my boyfriend?"

"Your boyfriend is a no-good, two-timing piece of shit."

"No, you did *not*." Beth wrapped her arms tighter around his neck, much like she had when we were kids, and I didn't envy Rick's position. She was a vicious little thing when provoked.

"What has gotten into you four?" Dad said, emerging from the house to see Rick pushing past me with Beth still latched on to him like a spider monkey.

"Help him," I managed, before I was sent flying backward into the snow. Thank God we had more than a few inches of padding, or we'd all have concussions at this point. I already planned on giving Rick one once he calmed his ass down. Jesus, he had it all wrong.

It was like Beth wasn't even there as Rick again dashed after Aiden, who led him on a wild chase around the perimeter of the yard, with Dad inserting himself into the mix to block Aiden.

"You need to move," Rick said to Dad, as he attempted to fake him out by going left.

"You need to stop trying to clobber our guests." Dad held his hands out, much the same as I'd done, but Rick faked him out again and managed to push past him. But this time, I was prepared, and seized Rick's ankle, and with as fast as he'd been running, the move sent him tumbling into the snow again, and that was the only thing that had Beth letting go.

"Hold him down," I yelled, crawling over to Rick, and before he could get up, I sat on his stomach, keeping him pinned down.

"All right, who do I need to knock out?" Mom said, flying out of the house with a frying pan held high.

Rick grabbed a handful of snow and shoved it in my face, and as I sputtered, I reached for my own handful and squashed it into his. He bucked up and rolled us over so he was on top of me, and then he began to pile the snow on top of me, burying me in it before clambering to his feet.

"You should all be thanking me," Rick shouted, and then looked over his shoulder to where Aiden stood by the tree across the yard—as far away from us as humanly possible. "If you knew what he did, you wouldn't be defending him."

As Rick was about to take off again, I struggled to sit up, trying to get to my feet so I could attempt to save Aiden from what was bound to be a hell of a beatdown, when I saw Holly's front door open a couple doors down.

Bundled up in the new red coat she'd bought on our last trip to the mall, she had a white beanie pulled down over her curls and a scarf to match, and as she looked in our direction, I swear to God I saw her eyebrows hit her hairline.

She jogged down the stairs as Rick took off again, and I scrambled to my feet. "Rick, you moron!" I shouted, hoping, by some miracle, he'd slip in the snow and fall on his ass. But no such luck. The boots he wore were apparently made for chasing down no-good, two-timing pieces of shit—or so he thought. Jesus, I'd always known my brother was pigheaded, but this was ridiculous, and so was he.

Holly made her way over to the yard, as Rick zipped by her, and when her eyes followed his path and landed on Aiden, they widened. "Oh my God. Aiden, you need to run."

My mom frowned. "Who's Aiden?"

"Watch out!" Holly shouted, moving her out of the way as Rick ran past.

Mom waved the frying pan in the air as she stalked after Rick. "You stop that chasing right now, or by God, I'll use this. I will!"

"Why don't you give that to me," Holly said, taking hold of one side, but Mom wasn't letting go.

"Do you see these boys? I might need it."

"You don't need it."

"I do."

As they played tug of war with the frying pan, I realized too late that Aiden wasn't running anymore. As a matter of fact, I couldn't see him anywhere at all, and then—

"Aiden!" I traipsed through the snow as fast as I could, to where Rick had grabbed hold of Aiden's legs and tackled him to the ground. Beth was yelling at him and doing all she could to pry him away, while Dad had Aiden's hands, pulling him in the opposite direction to get him loose from Rick's hold.

Everyone was yelling at everyone, even though half the family had no idea what was going on, when all of a sudden, a piercing whistle sounded from behind us, and we all froze. A cop car had stopped in front of the house without anyone noticing, and as the officer stepped out of the car, he dropped his whistle.

"Either this is the most twisted game of touch football I've ever seen, or we've got a problem here." He narrowed his eyes. "Is there a problem?"

I looked at Aiden, who looked at up at Dad, whose gaze landed on Rick—who was still practically spitting bullets in Aiden's direction.

Beth answered first as she got to her feet. "No problem here, officer. Just a fun family game, like you said." She glanced around, and then smacked Rick in the back. "Tag. You're it."

As she began to run off, the cop stepped in front of her and stopped her by the arms. "Whoa, young lady. I think maybe this 'game' of yours has seen enough excitement for the day." The cop gave a pointed look at my father. "Maybe you could have your family take it inside? Unless you'd like your neighbors calling me about a domestic disturbance? Can't promise I'd be this nice twice."

"No, that won't be necessary," my dad said, stepping forward with his hands up. "We're sorry for the disturbance." And then, in a commanding voice I hadn't heard since I was a teenager, he said, "Everyone to the living room. Now."

CHAPTER TWELVE

AIDEN

$\mathcal{W}$ ITH WARY EYES and heaving breaths, I watched the McAllister women head toward the front door as Holly dipped out of the fray back to her house.

Suzanne led the way with Beth trailing after her, and when Rick got to his feet, glaring at me, his father said, "Get going."

Rick's eyes narrowed on me, and he all but growled, but before he could say anything, Jack gave his shoulder a shove and said, "*Now*, Rick."

Rick turned on his heel and stomped through the snow to the door, his father following behind, and when Miles's eyes found mine, I could see apology swirling in the blue depths.

I was about to tell him it might be better if I just left, when Jack turned on the front stoop and said, "You two also. Inside, now."

As I ran a hand through my wet hair and swallowed, I wondered exactly what was about to happen now. Then Miles said under his breath, "Don't worry. It's all going to work out."

But really, how could it? I had lied to his entire family, and in about five minutes they were all going to know it. Oh well, at least we'd had one final kiss, right?

When we reached the living room, I found Suzanne now frying-pan-free and sitting by the fire in her recliner, Beth perched on the edge of it, and Rick standing with his arms crossed and his jaw clenched.

Jack stood beside his eldest son, as though ready to restrain him if the need again arose, and when Miles and I came to a standstill just inside the living room, Jack said, "Okay. Explain."

We all looked at each other, our lips tight, our wet clothes sticking to us, and then Rick said, "Maybe Beth's boyfriend should explain."

Beth sprang to her feet and balled her fists by her side. "Rick—"

Rick held up his hand and stared at Aiden. "*Well?* You care to tell her, or should I?"

"Tell me what?" Beth asked, shaking her head.

Not sure *what* Beth wanted me to say, I remained quiet, but that merely added ammunition to Rick's outrage.

"Your *boyfriend* here seems to be getting a little too close to our brother," Rick said, as he looked to where the two of us stood, and everyone's eyes widened.

Miles brought his hands to his face and groaned.

What a damn cluster—

"Sean?" Jack said. "Is that true?"

I looked at Beth, who sighed and got to her feet, rubbing her hands on her pants. "The truth is, I haven't been honest with you guys. Sean's not really my boyfriend."

Suzanne's mouth fell open as she looked at her daughter, and then she blinked a couple of times before getting to her feet.

"Look, I know you've been worried about me, and I just wanted to have a Christmas without all the questions about me still being single, or when will I have time for kids if I don't get married, and...I thought it would be easier this way."

Suzanne shook her head as though trying to get her mind around what her daughter was telling her, and then she looked at me and said, "So Sean is—"

"Someone I hired online," Beth said.

"*Online?*" Suzanne shrieked.

"Have you lost your mind, young lady?" Jack said as he aimed a pointed stare in his daughter's direction. "You don't know what kind of ingrates you'll find online. What if he'd been a serial killer? Did you think of that?"

I'm still here, I wanted to say, but thought it best that maybe they forgot that tidbit right now.

Beth sighed. "Well, obviously he's not, or we'd be chopped into bits already. I heard about him through a friend, so stop freaking out."

Rick shook his head. "You're insane."

"*I'm* insane? You're the one who's been hiding your secret girl-friend from everyone."

Rick's eyes widened, and his jaw close to hit the floor. He recovered quickly, though, and said, "Can we get back to the subject of a stranger in our house, please?"

"No, I don't think we can," Beth said, and crossed her arms, jutting her hip out to one side. "Hey, Mom, you remember Mrs. Wilkie, right?"

"Your high school math teacher?" Suzanne said. "What does she have to do with anything?"

Beth smirked at Rick like she'd won some kind of game. "That's who your son has been seeing."

"Rick!" Suzanne gasped, gaping at her eldest son. "Tell me that isn't true."

I had to admit it was kind of fun watching Rick squirm, as he tried to think of an excuse he could give to his mother, but when he clearly came up with nothing, Suzanne took a step toward him and said, "But...she's married!"

"She's separated," Rick said, and Miles scoffed, drawing my eye.

"Oh, Rick, what are you thinking?" Suzanne moaned and dropped her head in her hands.

"Uh, I'm still thinking who the hell that guy is," Rick said, pointing to me, and I tore my eyes away from Miles.

"Stop trying to change the subject," Beth said, and turned her attention to her mom. "Where do you think Rick's been sneaking off to all weekend?"

"I-I thought he was taking the cookies we made to the shelters," Suzanne said in a small voice.

Beth snorted. "That doesn't take five hours, Mom."

"How long have you been seeing Mrs. Wilkie?" Suzanne asked Rick.

"Can we not?" Rick said.

"Rick, answer your mother." Jack's tone was no-nonsense.

Rick let out a heavy sigh. "Five months. Okay? And it's not a big deal. She's not living with her husband anymore, and we like each other. So let's get back to the real issue here, which is Beth lying about her stranger-danger boyfriend here, who I caught kissing Miles out by the wood pile."

"Miles?" Suzanne said, and finally looked at her youngest son, who up until then had managed to keep out of the new bout of chaos that had taken over the McAllister household. "What on earth is he talking about? You were kissing...Sean?"

Miles opened his mouth, once, then twice, and when he looked to be struggling to find the right words, Suzanne spoke up again.

"So, Sean...*isn't* really Beth's boyfriend? And he was kissing *Miles*? I'm so confused," she said, and then sat back down.

Jack was shaking his head as he looked between his brood. "Who are you people? Certainly not the children I raised. Now would someone please explain who Sean is and why he's here?"

"Uh, well," I finally said, deciding I should probably try and defend myself in some way. "The first thing I should probably mention is my name isn't Sean."

"Oh, for the love of—" Rick said, but I quickly cut him short.

"Well, it is, but not the one I go by." I looked at Miles. "It's not the name Miles knows me by."

Miles smiled at me, and even though I felt as though my world was about to implode—that this strange but wonderful family was about to toss me out on my ass on Christmas Eve—that somehow made coming clean even more important.

Suzanne sighed, and when I turned back to face her, she said, "Would someone *please* straighten this out for me."

"Apparently that's the whole problem here, Mom," Rick said. "Straight isn't the way ol' Sean here swings."

"Shut up, you buffoon," Beth said. "Let the man talk. You know, something you weren't willing to do before you tried to pulverize his handsome face."

And just like that, five sets of eyes were all trained on me. "Uh, well, Miles and I met a couple of nights before I arrived here."

"Oh, you've got to be shittin'—"

"Zip it, son," Jack said to Rick.

"We bumped into each other at the mall, and then we ended up at a Christmas party together and hit it off. I had no idea he was related to Beth in any way at all."

"So"—Suzanne looked at Miles, who had remained silent —"Sean is the man you were talking about at lunch today? The man you'd just met?"

I looked at Miles, wondering what exactly he was going to say, and when his eyes met mine, he said, "Yes. But I know him as Aiden."

As I stared into Miles's beautiful face, I memorized everything about it, just in case this was the last time I saw it, then I looked back to his family. "That's right. I use Sean with my clients, like Beth, to keep things professional. I find that's the easiest way."

"And less sticky in situations like this," Rick piped up.

"There's never been a situation like this," I said, pinning Rick with a hard stare. "Not like Miles, and not like all of you."

"Beth is your...*client?*" Suzanne said, cocking her head to the side, the idea clearly a foreign one to her.

"Yes. As in, she hired me to come with her this weekend as her boyfriend."

"Oh my God," Beth said, and buried her face in her hands. "This is worse than when you all grill me about having kids." Then she dropped her hands down by her sides. "But seriously, can you see the lengths I am willing to go to, just to have you *not* talk about that?"

Suzanne looked so shocked by her daughter's outburst that I winced, and when she reached for Beth's hand, Beth shook her head.

"No," Beth said. "I don't want to talk about this right now." And before her mother could say anything else, Beth turned on her toes and ran up the stairs, away from the madness that had just unfolded.

Suzanne watched her daughter with a look of concern and confusion, as though she couldn't believe she had missed something so vital in her daughter's life, and I suddenly felt as though I was the light bulb shining the big, bright light over a very private and delicate situation.

"Uh, I think I'm gonna"—I gestured over my shoulder with my thumb—"go."

"You don't have to do that," Miles said, but there was no way I was going to stay. This family needed a moment, or three, to wrap their heads around what had happened, and me being there was not helping.

"Yeah, I do. I'm just going to get a hotel room or something." As I backed out of the living room, no one else tried to stop me. Miles reached for my hand, and as our fingers touched, I felt that spark, and I hoped to God that this wouldn't be the last time I saw him. And then I opened the front door and disappeared out into the cold, lonely afternoon.

CHAPTER THIRTEEN

MILES

I'D TOSSED AND turned all night. The thought of Aiden staying alone in a hotel on Christmas Eve bothered me, even more than my family learning the truth and the aftermath that had ensued. He didn't deserve that, not when all he was guilty of was being there to help my sister when she needed it. Sure, I'd complicated the situation unwittingly, but we'd all had good intentions. That had to count for something, right?

I flipped my pillow over so it was cool against my cheek again and settled back down on my side. Staring at the clock for the last half-hour hadn't made time go by any faster, and the minutes continued to tick by, slowly. When the time displayed seven a.m. on the dot, I threw off the covers and quickly dressed in a T-shirt and pajama pants. Then I opened the door and poked my head out into the hallway, listening for movement. All was still and quiet, so I tiptoed down to my old room and entered without a sound.

Beth lay still under the covers, but she was wide awake, and as I shut the door, it was obvious that she hadn't slept much either.

"May I?" I asked, gesturing at the empty side of the bed, and when she nodded, I climbed in beside her. "You okay?"

She sighed and sat up to lean against the headboard. "I'm okay. I feel bad about how all this went down, though. It's all my fault."

"It's not your fault."

"But it is. If I hadn't been so sensitive about things, I wouldn't have brought Sean here, and then I wouldn't have lied to everyone and ruined things for you and him too. God, I feel like a jinx."

"You're not a jinx. And you did what you had to do to protect yourself. Think of it this way: if Mom and Dad hadn't been on you so bad about the marriage and kids thing, you wouldn't have had to resort to doing what you did. So at least let them take some of the credit here."

"It's just so hard, you know? I feel this pressure, like hurry up and find someone, then hurry up and pop out a bunch of kids, but I need to do it now, now, now, or my body is basically gonna shrivel up and die. It's not enough that I have a decent job, my own apartment, and a thriving social life. I'm somehow inadequate because I'm not following the social norms."

"You're only inadequate in the kitchen."

She punched my arm. "Hey!"

"I'm kidding. But screw the norms. I am. Obviously Rick is." I knocked her shoulder with mine. "Hello, Mrs. Wilkie's a cradle robber, who knew?"

That earned me a tentative smile from Beth, and she wiped her eyes.

"You need to talk to Mom and Dad about how you feel," I said. "I knew they joked about it and it was annoying, but I don't think any of us really understood how much it bothered you. If they knew, I don't think they'd say anything."

"I don't want them thinking I'm disappointing them either. But I want different things. I'm not sure that kids fit into that picture."

"That's okay. Apparently Rick has super sperm, so I don't think our parents will lack for grandkids."

Beth burst out laughing and then clamped her hand over her mouth when it echoed off the walls.

"See? That can take the pressure off. Just talk to Mom and Dad. Promise?"

"Yeah. Yeah, I promise." Her eyes grew glassy, and a tear escaped the corner of her eye. "But Miles... I messed things up for you."

"No, you didn't. Rick the Ruiner did that all by himself."

A sad chuckle left her. "I can't believe he was seriously trying to attack Sean. Like what was that?"

"I think he was possessed. That's the only explanation. That or he's on some serious steroids."

Beth laughed harder at that and finally looked at me, resting her hand on my arm. "You need to find Sean and tell him how you feel."

"Beth—"

"No, I don't want to hear excuses. I have to have a talk, and now so do you. Sean's a good guy, and he deserves to know. And Miles? You deserve to be happy too. So if this guy makes you happy, don't let him go."

"Aww. When did you become such a romantic?"

"Since never, but it's Christmas. Maybe it's in the air or something. Tell you what, how about after breakfast and presents, I help you find where he went?"

That sounded like a fantastic idea, but there was one little problem: "I don't have his phone number."

Beth grinned and rolled over to reach for her phone on the nightstand, and then she scrolled through her contacts and held it out to me. "I do."

I took the cell from her, and sure enough, *Sean* and his phone number were right there. I took a deep breath. "Are you sure you're okay with this?"

"Miles," Beth said, and then flicked a finger over the hair that had flopped down across my forehead. "I'm positive. In fact, if you don't call him, I'll be pissed. The guy is seriously hot, not to mention sweet, and kind. Even Lucifer likes him. One of us should get him."

I nodded and threw the covers back, Beth's phone in hand. Maybe I could give him a quick call before we all went down—

Knock. Knock. Knock.

"Beth? Honey?" Mom's voice came through the door. "Are you awake?"

"Yeah, Mom," Beth said. "You can come in. Miles is here too."

As the door to my old bedroom pushed open, Mom stuck her head inside and looked between the two of us.

"This reminds me of when you were little kids," she said, a soft smile on her lips. "Always going into each other's rooms to wake the other one up."

I gave Beth her phone back, but made a mental note to get Aiden's number from her as soon as breakfast and presents were over, then I walked over to Mom and wrapped an arm around her shoulders. I could tell by the way she was talking that she was feeling emotional this morning, and I couldn't blame her— yesterday had been a lot to take for all of us.

"Some traditions never die," I said, then kissed her on the temple. "Just like I assume Rick is already downstairs shaking the boxes, am I right?"

She chuckled as she wound an arm around my waist. "I just told him to knock it off."

"Typical Rick," I said, and Mom nodded.

"Well, at least he seems to have relocated his brain and calmed down this morning." She then turned her eyes to Beth and said, "I think we all have."

Beth bit down on her lip and nodded, as Mom patted my back. "Miles? Do you mind giving me and you sister a moment alone? I'd like to talk to her about some things."

That was my cue. I gave Mom a final squeeze and shook my head. They needed this. And as I left the room, I looked back to see Mom sitting down on the edge of my old mattress and holding her arms out to Beth.

It was right then that I knew everything would be okay. If there was one thing I'd learned from growing up under the McAllister roof, it was that life could be chaotic and crazy, but as long as it was filled with a family who loved you, the craziness would eventually simmer down and love would win out in the end.

*A*FTER A CHRISTMAS breakfast that I was convinced I'd be full from for the rest of the day, the McAllister children were set to task, clearing away the plates, so we could then head to the living room and hand out the presents.

We took up our usual spots, with Mom in her recliner and Dad in his on the other side of the room, while I sat on the couch with Beth cross-legged on the rug beside me. Rick had his ridiculous Santa hat on, standing by the tree, and as I looked at the fireplace where our stockings all hung filled to bursting, I couldn't help but feel a pang of regret at seeing the sixth one Mom had hung for Aiden.

What was he doing this morning? I had no idea. He'd told us all that he didn't get along with his family, so I knew he wasn't on the phone with them, or sitting by a tree smiling with them like we all were, now that the storm had passed—and that...that made my heart ache.

I wished he was right there with us, sitting beside me, where I could hold his hand, smell his cologne, and watch his eyes crinkle at the sides when he smiled. But instead he was likely sitting in a cold, empty hotel room, thinking me and my family were the biggest Grinches around.

As Rick began passing out our stockings, we each took them from him. First Mom and Dad, followed by Beth, and then finally he took mine from the hook and handed it to me. We hadn't really said much to one another this morning, but it was understood we'd all behaved badly, and it was time to let bygones be bygones.

But when I reached for my stocking, Rick said, "Hey, Miles?"

I raised an eyebrow at his chagrined expression. "Yeah?"

"Sorry for being such a dipshit yesterday."

I let out a bark of laughter and shrugged. "It's all good."

"Nah, I scared off your man... Well, Beth's man. Whatever. And I'm sorry."

I nodded, as he finally let go of the stocking. "Thanks. Sorry I had to tackle you a couple times."

Rick snorted. "You were pretty good, bro. I'm impressed." He clapped me on the shoulder. "Just don't do it again."

We all laughed as he snagged his stocking and plopped down on the couch beside me. My eyes caught again on the lone stocking hanging off the mantel, and I had the same sense of unease I'd felt all morning whenever Aiden crossed my mind. It didn't feel right celebrating without him. I didn't like the thought of him being alone today of all days, and I...missed him.

"Um, do you mind giving me a few minutes? I need to make a phone call," I said, moving my stocking to the side so I could stand. Beth looked up at me and, without me having to ask, pointed toward the kitchen.

"I left my phone on the counter," she said, but no sooner were the words out of her mouth than the doorbell rang.

Hope leapt into my throat at the possibility of Aiden being on the other side of that door, but then Mom said, "Is that Holly? She never could wait long before seeing what you got for Christmas."

Oh. Oh, right. I swallowed, nodding, the probability of our visitor being my best friend much higher than the man who'd all but been run out yesterday. Not that I wouldn't be happy to see Holly—we had so much to talk about, and I'd only been able to give her a brief rundown of what Aiden was doing there when she stopped by to steal a few of my mom's sweet treats.

"Miles? Are you gonna get that?" Beth asked.

I nodded again as I made my way toward the door, running my hand through my bedhead. After unlocking the deadbolt, I swung the door wide, only to find that it wasn't my best friend standing on the porch step at all.

It was Aiden.

And just as it always did when I saw him, my heart rate kicked up, bringing a warm heat to my body even with the cold wind whipping around us. He looked beautiful as ever with the heavier stubble covering his cheeks and his ebony hair blowing across his forehead, and I wanted to reach out and push it back from his face. His hands were shoved inside the pockets of the same jeans he'd been wearing yesterday, though his clothes looked like they'd been washed and pressed since then. Of course he was wearing the same outfit. Aiden hadn't exactly gotten a chance to grab his bag before he'd left.

"Hi," he said, giving me a tight smile. It wasn't one I'd ever been on the receiving end of before, and I didn't like it. It felt too polite, too forced.

"Hi. Merry Christmas."

He inclined his head, his dark eyes carrying a sadness that hit me square in the chest. "Merry Christmas. I didn't mean to interrupt. I won't be long. I just wanted to grab my bag so I can get on the road."

"Wh-what? You're leaving? Now?"

"Yeah. Avoid the traffic rush tomorrow and all."

Dammit. That wasn't the real reason, and we both knew it.

"I missed you." It came out of my mouth before I knew I was going to say it, but I didn't regret it, not one bit, because it was true. I loved my family, but there was an obvious empty space where Aiden should've been this morning. Where he should be now.

Aiden's eyebrows shot up, and he swallowed before looking away. "I missed you too," he said, so quietly I almost missed it.

As I took a step toward him, the door behind me flung wide open, and my mom appeared.

"Well, for heaven's sake, Miles, don't make him stand out there and freeze to death. Come in, dear. Get warm."

I moved aside so Aiden could go in first, and as he entered, his gaze landed on the happy family scene in the living room, and he said, "Sorry to intrude. I'll just grab my things." As he headed for the stairs, my dad sprang out of his chair.

"Sean, one second, please," Dad said, as he came to a stop by the banister. "Look, we owe you an apology. The whole family does." He swept his hand in our direction, and we all nodded and a chorus of "I'm sorry" rang out.

"We're really not this dysfunctional all the time," Beth said, coming up beside Dad, and then she paused and looked back at Rick. "Well, that one is."

Rick put his hands up. "Okay, okay, I'll admit, I was a little rough yesterday, but I was defending my sister's honor, you feel me? Nobody messes with my family."

"Hey, doofus," I said. That's not an apology."

"I'm getting there." Rick shot me a look before turning back to Aiden. "I'm sorry, man. I should've let you and Miles explain what you were...doing."

"Thank you. I appreciate your apology." Aiden shook the hand Rick proffered, and then Rick clapped him on the arm as he stepped away. Two seconds later, he was running his mouth again.

"But seriously, you two should've waited until you weren't Beth's 'boyfriend' anymore, know what I'm sayin'?" Rick said.

Beth rolled her eyes and pushed him back toward the living room. "Okay, that's enough outta you."

"I'd like to apologize too," Mom said, stepping forward. "Do you prefer to go by Sean or Aiden?"

"I go by Aiden to my friends and loved ones." Aiden's eyes met mine briefly, but it was enough to see the spark that told me his feelings hadn't changed in the hours since we'd last seen each other.

"Well, Aiden, it's nice to officially meet you. And to add to what the others have said, we all behaved atrociously yesterday. That's what happens when you jump to conclusions and don't listen. To think that you had to stay in a hotel by yourself on Christmas Eve because of us—" Her words got stuck as she choked up and pulled a tissue out of a box nearby. "I just want to say I'm sorry...and thank you."

"Thank me for what?" Aiden said, his forehead creased.

"You were there when my Beth needed you and we weren't

listening. Jack and I were wrong to try to force something on her that she doesn't want, and you helped make us see that. So thank you. You're a good man, Sean. Sorry—Aiden."

As Mom stepped forward and wrapped her arms around Aiden's waist, hugging him tight, he stood there rigid, surprise written all over his face. Like he didn't know what to do with her outpouring of affection, or maybe it was the apology she'd given. His gaze fell on me, and I gave him an encouraging smile. If he didn't have a family, then he could share mine, for as long as he wanted to.

As if he'd wanted my permission, Aiden hugged Mom back, and she squeezed him tighter before letting him go.

Aiden cleared his throat as he looked around at us, looking more nervous than I'd ever seen him. He was always the picture of cool, calm, and collected, but we'd knocked him off balance somehow, and I had a feeling he wasn't sure what to do next.

"I, um... I really appreciate you all for saying those things. But I owe you all an apology, too. I came here under false pretenses, and I expected the job to be just that—a job. Obviously it turned into more than that. You all welcomed me into your family without a second thought and made me feel more at home than I have in years. I'll never forget that. So thank you, too."

"Oh, sweetheart," Mom said, dabbing at her eyes. "Gracious, you're making this old woman cry all her mascara off already. Are you hungry? We've got so much food left over from breakfast—"

Aiden shook his head. "No, ma'am, I need to be getting on the road, but thank you for the offer."

Mom took a step toward him and jabbed him in the chest. "If you haven't been paying attention, you're not going anywhere, so you just climb back down here and join us for Christmas."

"Oh no, I couldn't do that—"

"Miles," Mom said, waving me over. "How about you convince Aiden to stay while we go get the hot cocoa ready?"

"But we already made some earlier," Rick said, not picking up on the hint.

"And it's probably cold, so we'll have to make some again," she said, heading for the kitchen with Beth as Jack pulled Rick off the back of the couch by his shirt collar.

And then Aiden and I were alone. Well, as alone as we could be in this crazy household. I inclined my head toward the living room, and he followed me to where the massive tree stood, its lights sparkling because of Aiden.

"Miles, I—"

I brought my fingers up to his lips, which were soft to the touch. "Let me go first." When he nodded, I dropped my hand and wanted to reach for his but held myself back. "I know this has been a wild weekend, one you didn't realize you signed up for. But I don't regret it, because it forced us to get to know each other better than we would've on a polite first date."

Aiden's eyes sparkled as he laughed, and that was all the incentive I needed to touch him again. I laced our fingers together, and that part of me that had been missing earlier clicked back into place.

"I don't blame you if you want to leave," I said. "But I'd really like you to stay."

He brushed his thumb over my hand, and I squeezed. "You want me to stay?" he said.

"Mhmm," I said, as an idea sprang to mind. "In fact, I think we should start over, right back at the beginning."

I gave him a cheeky grin and, without letting go of his hand, led him to the large bay window that overlooked the front yard. Snow fell in light flurries, and from where we stood, the entire neighborhood looked like a winter wonderland.

"It's beautiful," Aiden said.

My eyes roamed over his exquisite face. "It is."

Aiden met my stare, and then I pointed above us, and when he saw what was there, he let out a loud laugh.

"A fresh start, huh?" he said. "I think I like the sound of that."

"Good. Because it was either this mistletoe or a Three Wise Men shot."

"Well, we both know I've developed a sweet tooth." Aiden cradled my face, and I moved up onto my toes to meet him halfway.

"Merry Christmas," I whispered right before his lips touched mine, and when they met, I closed my eyes and clutched at his arm for support.

My knees shook, and my body trembled, and just like it had from the very beginning, that magical feeling swirled around us. That spark of instant awareness.

"Merry Christmas, Miles," Aiden said against my mouth, and as we stood there beneath the mistletoe, I had a feeling this wouldn't be the last time I heard him say those three words to me. This was the man I was supposed to meet. I knew that right down to my very soul. This was fate.

EPILOGUE

MILES

One Year Later...

"**M**ERRY CHRISTMAS, MILES."

My eyes opened at the deep voice in my ear, and as I stretched my legs beneath the sheets, a strong arm wrapped around my waist.

"Mmm, merry Christmas," I said, sleep making my voice lazy as I snuggled into the warm arms enveloping me. "This is much better than the way I woke up last year."

Full lips nuzzled in under my ear, and when a chuckle made the body behind me vibrate, I knew Aiden was thinking the same thing. "You don't say."

"I do," I said, and turned my head to stare at the man who was stretched out behind me in my childhood queen-sized bed—exactly where he should've been all along.

Aiden's lips curved into the gorgeous smile that had first swept me off my feet, and when I rolled in his arms so I was facing him, he shifted to make room for me.

"You look good in my bed, Mr. Mahoney." I tangled my bare

legs with his pajama-clad ones to keep nice and toasty, and moved in closer so my head was resting on the same pillow as his.

"I'm glad you think so. Your floor is really uncomfortable."

"I wouldn't know."

"I would, trust me. And I don't ever want to end up there again."

I brushed a kiss against his lips. "Never..."

"Hmm, good. 'Cause I kind of like it right here."

And so did I. This past year had been the best of my life, and that was due largely in part to the man who was now trailing his fingers down my cheek, and looking at me as though I'd hung the moon.

Not a day had gone by, since he'd shown back up on my parents' doorstep, that we didn't see or talk with one another, and as the months had passed, our relationship had progressed to the point where we were now going to officially start looking for a place together.

Truth be told, I probably would've jumped into that decision much sooner than now, but there'd been no way I was about to leave Holly in the lurch without a roommate to take my place. But ever since she'd gotten her fancy new promotion, at Kloss Fashion House, she'd been talking about looking for a place to call her own.

Whether that was because she actually *wanted* to be Miss Independent, or she was just sick of watching the way Aiden and I mooned all over one another, I wasn't sure. But either way, I felt better knowing she was moving up in the world, as I moved out.

It looked as though Santa had really come through for her on that wish of hers, and speaking of Santa...

"Hey?" I said, and bit my lower lip.

There was something that had been niggling in the back of my mind ever since I'd dragged Aiden along with me and Holly for our now-traditional "sit on Santa's lap photo" last weekend.

I'd debated bringing it up with him, wondering if he'd think I was deranged. But after last night's conversation at dinner about the time I'd put tape on Rick's eyebrows and gave him a semipermanent wax job, I figured it was a safe assumption that Aiden was here to stay.

"Yeah?"

"You know how I told you about that wish I made last year, with Santa?"

Aiden shifted back a little and propped his head on his hand. "I do. You told me you wished for me."

I nodded. "Right. Well, wished for 'a boyfriend,' if we're getting technical."

"Oh? So it could've been anyone? Good to know." Aiden laughed, and I shoved his rumbling chest. He took hold of my wrist and brought my hand up to kiss the back of my hand.

"No," I said. "I just made it...generic."

"Mhmm, okay," Aiden said, and my heart sped up, as it always did when he focused on me.

How is he mine? There really was only one explanation that made sense, wasn't there?

"Well, when we got our photo taken this year, do you remember, as we were leaving, Santa called me back?"

"Yeah, he whispered something in your ear that you refused to tell me."

I gnawed on my lip. "I didn't want you to think I was crazy, that's why."

Aiden's brows rose. "Why would I think you were crazy?"

"Because what I didn't tell you about last year was that when I visited Santa, I saw you across the mall and I had this thought."

"Ooh, I'm liking this," Aiden said with a naughty grin.

"Not that kind of thought. Thank God. Because Aiden...I think Santa read my mind. I think he's real."

Aiden's shock was clearly written all over his face, and before he could tell me I was insane, I hurried on.

"I saw you, and I remember thinking, clear as a bell, *You put that guy under my Christmas tree this year, and I'll happily eat my words.* And you know what Santa said to me this year?"

Aiden's eyes narrowed.

"He said, 'Well, I put him under your tree for you, young man. Now it's up to the both of you where you go from here.'" And just like when Santa said it to me, goosebumps broke out all over my skin.

When Aiden said nothing, I screwed my nose up. "Do you think I'm nuts? Are you wondering what you're doing lying in bed with some guy who still believes in Santa? Who thinks he *actually* had a conversation with Santa...twice?"

Aiden cradled my cheek and pressed a soft, sweet kiss to my lips. "Thank you."

I put my hands to his chest and scooted in closer to him. "Thank you?"

Aiden gave me an Eskimo kiss, and then leaned his forehead to mine, shut his eyes, and whispered, "For wishing for me."

My eyes welled at the love I could hear in his voice. "Best wish I've ever made."

Aiden's eyes opened. "Yeah?"

"Definitely," I said, and then heard myself say, "I love you, Sean Aiden Mahoney."

Never had words felt more right, and when Aiden whispered, "I love you too, Miles Graham McAllister," I melted into his embrace and added this moment to the other perfect ones that had come before this, knowing there'd be plenty more in our future.

Especially if Santa came through with *this* year's wish. -wink-

THANK YOU

Thank you for reading! We hope you enjoyed this fun, romantic Christmas tale.

If you did, please consider leaving a review on the site you purchased the book from.

Still in a holiday mood?
Check out our other Christmas short story, Wrapped Up in You, coming soon to PassionFlix.

ALSO BY BROOKE BLAINE

South Haven Series

A Little Bit Like Love

A Little Bit Like Desire

The Unforgettable Duet

Forget Me Not

Remember Me When

L.A. Liaisons Series

Licked

Hooker

P.I.T.A.

Romantic Suspense

Flash Point

PresLocke Series

Co-Authored with *Ella Frank*

Aced

Locked

Wedlocked

Standalone Novels

Co-Authored with *Ella Frank*

Sex Addict

Shiver

Wrapped Up in You

Thanos

Standalones

Blind Obsession

Veiled Innocence

Co-Authored with Brooke Blaine

Sex Addict

Shiver

Wrapped Up in You

PresLocke Series
Co-Authored with Brooke Blaine

ACED

LOCKED

WEDLOCKED

ABOUT BROOKE BLAINE

About Brooke

Brooke Blaine is a *USA Today* Bestselling Author of contemporary and LGBT romance that ranges from comedy to suspense to erotic. The latter has scarred her conservative Southern family for life, bless their hearts.

If you'd like to get in touch with her, she's easy to find - just keep an ear out for the Rick Astley ringtone that's dominated her cell phone for years. Or you can reach her at www.Brooke-Blaine.com.

Brooke's Links
Brooke's Newsletter
Brooke & Ella's Naughty Umbrella
Book + Main Bites

www.BrookeBlaine.com
brooke@brookeblaine.com

ABOUT ELLA FRANK

If you'd like to get to know Ella better, you can find her getting up to all kinds of shenanigans at:

The Naughty Umbrella

And if you would like to talk with other readers who love Robbie, Julien & Priest, you can find them at
Ella Frank's Temptation Series Facebook Group.

Ella Frank is the *USA Today* Bestselling author of the Temptation series, including Try, Take, and Trust and is the co-author of the fan-favorite contemporary romance, Sex Addict. Her Exquisite series has been praised as "scorching hot!" and "enticingly sexy!"

Some of her favorite authors include Tiffany Reisz, Kresley Cole, Riley Hart, J.R. Ward, Erika Wilde, Gena Showalter, and Carly Philips.

Want to stay up to date with all things Ella?
You can sign up here to join her newsletter

For more information
www.ellafrank.com

Made in the USA
Middletown, DE
15 August 2019